P9-DDS-515

SEVEN FOR A SECRET

SEVEN FOR A SECRET

ॐ

Mary C. Sheppard

A Groundwood Book
Douglas & McIntyre
Toronto Vancouver Berkeley

Groundwood Books/Douglas & McIntyre
720 Bathurst Street, Suite 500, Toronto, Ontario M5S 2R4

Distributed in the USA by Publishers Group West
1700 Fourth Street, Berkeley, CA 94710

We acknowledge the financial support of the Canada Council for the Arts,
the Ontario Arts Council and the Government of Canada through the
Book Publishing Industry Development Program
for our publishing activities.

ONTARIO ARTS COUNCIL
CONSEIL DES ARTS DE L'ONTARIO

National Library of Canada Cataloging in Publication Data

Sheppard, Mary C. (Mary Catherine)
Seven for a secret
ISBN 0-88899-507-5
Title.
PS8587.H38533S48 2002   jC813'.54
C2002-900140-4
PZ7.S53Se 2002

Design by Michael Solomon
Cover illustration by Stephanie Power
Printed and bound in Canada

For Paul, Melanie and Rebecca-Anne

and for my parents
Mary and George S. Sheppard

One for sorrow
Two for joy
Three for a wedding
Four for a boy
Five for silver
Six for gold
Seven for a secret that can't be told

CHAPTER ONE

❧

A woman's tongue is her sword

When Kate arrived from the city in June it was always my job
to yank her off the ferry and get her set to rights the second
she crossed the gangplank to the government wharf.

This past summer was no different. That was one of the
few things that didn't change.

"Come on, Kate," I said. "Are you waitin' till the sea runs
dry?"

She got off the *Irene L.* wearing an awful pink dress.
Straight from the Eaton's catalogue, it was, but the dress desperately needed darts and tucks so it didn't just droop over her
scrawny body. I grabbed her hand and her bag, which
weighed a ton, and pulled her along the main drag, the only
real road in Cook's Cove.

"Be careful of my books. I brought all the Jane Austens,"
said Kate.

Kate and her books. She always had her nose in one and
she was beginning to know my hiding places for them.

"Wave to old Johnny Pumphrey, the old flirt. No teeth

and blind as a bat he is. Must be half cracked if he gets excited seeing you," I said. I wiggled my backside, gave him a brazen smile and sang out for his ancient ears, "Hey, good lookin', whatcha got cookin?" Johnny flashed us a toothless grin and we fluttered our hands without breaking our stride. We were practically running along the Cove road but my mouth managed to keep up.

"Don't look now 'cause Millie's hiding behind her lace curtain. She's some stunned if she thinks we can't see her. Her picture window is only a foot off the road, Lord dyin'. Do you like my hair long or should I cut it? You need to cut your bangs, Kate, and take in that dress if you're going to wear it to the garden party. Lordy, did you see that? Annie Lake was just about to hang out her corsets and step-ins but she put them back in the basket when she saw you. She likes to let city folk think she is so proper. Don't be too friendly, Kate, she'll be all over us. Why are you so quiet?"

I paid no mind to Kate's wide-eyed look and we had a good giggle. Getting her off the boat got to be my duty because I was the only one saucy enough to just ignore everyone who wanted to have a little gossip with Kate, this her first day in Cook's Cove since last fall. Straight from the big city in the Bay, Corner Brook, she was. People off the boat had to be offered a cup of tea the instant their feet hit dry land. That was our God-given obligation. I always pushed Kate along so us cousins could have our tea without a dozen tongues flapping on about how much we had grown and all that nonsense.

"Hello, Mrs. Lake. No, I can't stop for tea right now. I'll come by soon," said Kate as I jabbed a finger between her ribs.

Five minutes off the boat I pushed Kate's battered suitcase into the corner behind Aunt Grace's side door and we went into the house to find Rebecca. We had been together for eight summers, from the lilacs in June right through to the second blooming of our climbing roses in September. I was the oldest and Kate was the youngest but there were only seven months separating the three of us. We'd been best cousins since Kate, a sickly child, started coming out here for the fresh sea air. I practically grew up with my other cousin, Rebecca. Me and Rebecca always made a fuss of Kate when she arrived in the Cove for the summer. We'd gone from tea with our teddies and dolls to last year's white gloves and feather hats like in the Hollywood films.

No hats this year but all three of us were gussied up in our Sunday best. I was wearing my yellow sundress that fit snugly in all the right places and Rebecca was in one of her navy cotton dresses with pearl buttons up the front and a sprig of everlasting forget-me-nots tucked into the Peter Pan collar.

We ran straight into one of Aunt Grace's Ladies' Aid meetings. The ladies were cheek by jowl around the kitchen table and my aunt was assigning them their jobs. Kate got a hurried near-hug from our aunt and Grace's cool red lips barely touched her cheek but it was enough to set us free. Aunt Grace didn't kiss me, of course—just gave me a long look that said something like, "No trouble from you today, you hear, young lady." Imagine.

Rebecca lived Down Below. That's what we called the place where the houses were huddled on the beach. It was where the first houses were built in the Cove. Their house backed onto the breakwater smack in the middle of the crescent of the shoreline.

Uncle Wilf had long been the best fisherman this end of the Bay of Islands. He worked long and hard and he knew his fish. Aunt Grace was the social be-all in Cook's Cove and for a few miles around too. She ran all the church committees, because she'd worked in a hospital during the war, she tended to our sicknesses. She was someone you wouldn't want to cross. Aunt Grace was forever giving Rebecca a hard time, telling her to sit up straight, eat her tinned peas, not slosh her tea, put out her lamp, say her prayers, down her cod liver oil, move her bowels once a day. Aunt Grace spoke softly and always smiled but she had the Derby bossy trait and an iron hand. Yes siree!

Rebecca was just setting the china teapot and the fancy floral cups and saucers on the mahogany side table when we stepped into the parlor. She'd spent the morning folding white linen luncheon napkins, arranging lilacs, baking chocolate-toffee squares and cutting dainty egg salad sandwiches made with store-bought bread. She had even unearthed the blue Wedgwood that came on the boat with the first Derbys a couple of lifetimes ago. Little Miss Homemaker 1960.

I snatched a chocolate-toffee square before she had time to take off the wax paper.

"These are some shockin' good," I sputtered, even though I knew I shouldn't be talking with my mouth full.

"We have napkins, my maid. We're not heathens and you're not a gannet. Sit down and eat like a Christian," said Rebecca.

I pinched the biggest one on the plate and stuffed it straight down my gob while Rebecca reached for the teapot.

"Sacred Heart of the Mother of Jesus. I'm starvin'," I moaned. "Been up scrubbing since six this morning. Oh my son. All for you, Kate. Mom and Nan would hate for you to see how we really live. I was on my hands and knees with a can of paste wax and Mom was practically crackin' a whip."

"As if your mom can make you do anything you don't want to do. I'd like to see the day," said Rebecca.

Folks here have always told me I talk a lot. My family, and

especially my two cousins, would tell me to shut my lip or roll their eyes when my tongue got going. Sometimes they even walked away while I had words hurting my mouth with their need to be born.

I never paid them no heed. In a small place like Cook's Cove, population four hundred and zippo, where we didn't see outsiders all winter and we had to make up our own fun, there was always something to be overheard or made up to be spread around. They always waited with their tongues hanging out. Just in case I had something juicy.

"Which reminds me," I said. "I've got to catch you up on my Matt and me. We're basically engaged but Mom won't let me wear a ring. He bought a to-die-for diamond last winter at Alteen's in the city but he's keeping it until Mom lets me wear it. I'm working on her. She gets this determined look on her face, shakes her head, clenches her teeth and says I have to finish high school. Lord jumpin' dyin', another year! I'll be an old maid by the time I finish grade eleven. Rebecca will go off to teachers' college and I'll be pining away, waxing floors, the only unmarried spinster over the age of sixteen. My Matt is building our house this summer. Do you like this new lipstick? It's Hot Fever. Chas broke up with Polly last week. She's as ugly as sin since she had all her teeth pulled out. A mouthful of rotten teeth. Can you imagine kissing someone with no teeth?"

"Melinda," Kate said, "you've got a one-track mind." She was right. I snatched another square to make up for my sins.

My cousins liked my Matt. They always said we were a perfect match. He was so calm and quiet while I was the social one. But they squirmed whenever I said the marriage word. I'd already heard a hundred times their plans to go to university and they kept nudging how I should be thinking along those lines too. The talk in the Cove was that I would be some nurse because I had a knack for looking after sick people.

They changed the conversation away from boys to music and books and my mind wandered.

What you got to picture here is that we were in Aunt Grace's parlor. The best room in Cook's Cove. Kate and I were sitting on a wine-colored, stiff-backed chesterfield that had white lace doilies on the arms and the back. Rebecca was sitting on a three-corner green-striped silk chair. The rug was swirls of red roses smothered in green leaves and yellow love knots.

They were yakking away but I had to get up. I couldn't sit still in such a fussy room. As I let my fingers wander over the worn keys of the walnut piano, the painting hung over it caught my eye. It was all smudges of greens and blues that when you stood back became a pretty stream flowing around a pair of birch trees and into the sea. I wasn't one for arty stuff but even I liked this one. It reminded me of the brook up behind our house. We even had overhanging birch trees in about the same place. Rebecca, who drew sketches all the time, liked to go on about how perfect it was.

"It's not easy to get the brush strokes so relaxed and yet have so much energy," she told us, and Kate and I nodded like we knew what she was talking about. Not a clue between us.

I turned to face the room. None of the fancy furniture in the parlor was from Eaton's. It was solid and hand-carved. My Aunt Grace used to live in Boston and while she didn't talk much about her time there, everyone in the Cove saw the fancy furniture come off the boat when she came back. She went there during the war as a nurse's helper and came home a few years later after marrying Uncle Wilf in Halifax. He was from the Cove too but was in the navy. They tried to make a go of it in Halifax but Uncle Wilf wasn't too well after the war and he missed his fishing. That's how Rebecca got to be born on the mainland. But she wasn't stuck-up about it.

All the fancy tables in the parlor were covered with framed photographs. Some of the older frames were downright ugly—done up with loops of hair tied in fancy knots glued onto varnished wood. The more recent photos were in heavy silver frames that Aunt Grace ordered special from the jewelry shops in Corner Brook and even from St. John's.

The photos in the hairy frames were taken by traveling men who came to Cook's Cove over the years. There was a picture of Great-Grandfather and Great-Grandmother dressed in their wedding clothes in 1900. Great-Grandmother Evie looked big and strong in the picture but she didn't live long, dead by the time my nan was fourteen. A hard life she had, living across the harbor with a man who never understood that a woman liked company. Close by was the picture of Nan and Grandfather Derby, also in wedding clothes, in 1916—she a wisp of a girl, he a grown man in full beard.

The biggest hairy photo was taken around 1928. It was of Nan and Granddad—now Captain Derby with his own fleet of schooners—and the children. Herb was standing between his parents, already a big ten-year-old, and Grace, a year older, looking beautiful and solemn, a princess dressed in velvet and silk ribbons. And my mom, Mae, just a baby sitting on Nan's lap dolled up in a long white christening grown and a lace cap. The perfect family. Good thing they got the traveling man to take the photo that summer. That fancy life didn't last long.

The grandest silver picture was the one of my Aunt Grace. It was taken in the forties in Boston and is touched up in color. She looks like one of those glamour queens you see in the Hollywood magazines. Her head is tilted and her wavy blond hair falls down her back. Another small photo was of my aunt dressed in her Red Cross uniform and standing between two thin men whose faces were just gray blurs. The men, one in a dark suit, the other in uniform, were two of her patients, she told us. There was a photo of Aunt Grace holding Rebecca, my cousin's face pressed onto her shoulder, a studio picture done in Halifax. And Uncle Wilf holding Rebecca on his lap while Aunt Grace is standing alongside his shoulder.

Uncle Wilf was a fine-looking man with a head full of dark curls, dark blue eyes and laugh lines as deep as a creek. The man was close to six and a half feet tall. Aunt Grace was no shrinking violet herself at close to six feet. The blue eyes and the height ran in the Derby family and my aunt and uncle were both Derbys—second cousins in fact.

There was a picture of my mom and dad too but we had the same one on our sideboard in the dining room, so I didn't spend much time looking at it. It was their wedding day and they looked to be the happiest couple alive.

There was a collection of seven photos of weddings taken from 1955 to 1959, mostly with a white church in the background. Kate had seven sisters, and whenever one got married, she dutifully sent Aunt Grace a photo for her tables. I was hoping my photo would be there by the fall.

While I was doing the family tour Kate and Rebecca jabbered on about the wonders of sliced bread, music that wasn't country and western and provincial school exams. The two morons were so excited about the results, talking endlessly about the history question on page three that might have brought their marks down two points. Ye gods! As far as I was concerned, whatever marks we got, we got. It was too late to worry now and we'd find out in August anyway.

Rebecca was a bit of a teacher's pet. She did her work and

showed up my bad work habits to no end. Only the two of us did grade ten up at the school last year so it was easy for the teacher to see who was doing what. I finally had to hit the books to get her off my God-fearing back. My Matt didn't like it one bit. When I was studying there was no time for necking out behind the shed.

When Rebecca was not scrubbing floors for her mom or for the church or blackening the top of their new woodstove or eating her baked beans, she was down at the stage helping her dad clean the fish or spread it out to dry on the flakes. There weren't too many girls who helped out with the fishing anymore, but Rebecca lived for it. She had a real soft spot for her old man. When you saw the two heads bobbing and them talking softly over the splitting table or the salt barrels, you'd have thought they were brothers. They were both dark, showing traces of Micmac and French ancestors. They were different in that he was craggy and she was smooth, he was tall and square and she was tall and slender. But they were alike in the way they leaned into the table, their hands moving to the same rhythm as they flicked out a liver or cut out a jowl, and in the way their bodies draped against a wooden fish barrel when they sat down to jag on the stage. Doing the fish, they could talk for hours. At home, with Aunt Grace hovering and fussing, there were few words spared.

There were plans for Rebecca to be the first girl in the Cove to go to university in St. John's, clear across the island. Aunt Grace had her heart set on Rebecca being a teacher up at the school. My cousin didn't seem to care about boys. But she was pretty and I reckoned those jewel eyes and the glossy black braid down to her arse, not to mention the 34-D bustline, might put the teaching plan in a spin.

I was getting restless. The chocolate in the squares made me over-anxious for a smoke and a bottle of Coke. I picked the last of the toffee from between my teeth and broke up the party. It was time to get my city cousin moving. I desperately needed to visit the outhouse to suck back on an Export A.

We lived in the old family home that sat on the hill where we could see our Cove, the whole harbor and even a bit out along the Bay on a clear day. I expected my mom and Nan would live there until they were carried out in coffins. Our end of the Cove was called Upalong, because that's where it was, away from the beach, on a hill. My daddy, the man who would listen to me talk forever while I helped him stack the cod and who took me away from the never-ending housework, drowned when his dory capsized in a nasty squall. I was ten and that was five years ago. It was so hard when he died. Me and Mom and my little twin brother and sister, Georgie and Flossie, all moved back in with Nan when our savings ran out. My mom didn't want to sponge on the welfare so she worked in the fish plant for six or seven months every year and got the dole in the winter. Nan's house was once the Big House in Cook's Cove but it got to be a little worn out. Like Mom.

Rebecca and Kate took their time saying goodbye. Moving Kate out of the parlor, I had to look at her pink dress again. I had drooled over it on the model in the spring catalogue.

Darling dress in nylon sheer with an all-over white velvety pin dot pattern. Bodice is rayon taffeta lined. A sewn-in taffeta slip. Shoulders-wide collar prettied with band of tiny box pleats all-'round. Bouffant skirt gathered all-'round at waist; self belt to wear if you wish. $12.98.

Good thing she was wearing the belt because she was a beanpole, and the belt made her look a little less ridiculous.

"Mom said I had to buy this darn thing. As soon as I turned fifteen in the spring she's been on my back about how grand it would be for me to have a fella. She thinks this dress is bait," Kate said as we headed for the side door.

I worked real hard at holding my tongue. Bouffant did not work on a girl with no waist, no hips and no bust. She had nice eyes. That much was true. Lots of us in the Derby crowd had her cornflower blues. And she had pretty feet. There was a deep hollow just behind her anklebone that was as delicate as a buttercup. But the hair was another story. It was thick and blond, which was good, but it was always tied back in a droopy ponytail with an elastic band at the nape of her skinny neck and it was often full of tats because she never took out the elastics at night. No one had seen her amazing eyes in years. Her bangs were one big cowlick. They were always too long and the way she constantly pushed them to the left was not pretty. And she wore these cat's-eye glasses with gold scrolls across the rim. I was desperate to scoot her up the hill and get her into her old baggy blue jeans before anyone saw this vision of delight.

I suggested to Kate that it was getting chilly and she borrowed one of Uncle Wilf's huge Aran sweaters and pranced up the main drag and the lane to our house. I was trying to get in a puff or two on my Export A but my goody-goody cousin, who went to a school taught by the nuns, was scared senseless I would get caught smokin' in broad daylight. Thanks to Kate, I finally had to crush a long butt into my hand. She just wouldn't shut up about me getting into trouble.

Kate grew up in the city but was innocent as a herring heading toward a net. Her dad, my Uncle Herb, moved away from Cook's Cove when he was a barely grown boy. The fishing was god-awful, my grandpa had died and Nan needed cash or face another hungry winter. No matter how many times the family had bread and salt fish for dinner, or no fish at all, our nan could not make the flour and fish last no more than January. I've heard the tale on many a dark night sitting around the woodstove in any number of warm kitchens.

Uncle Herb got a job at the paper mill in the town at the head of the Bay of Islands and he stayed. He married a Catholic so there was no use him ever planning to come back. The town became a city and Kate and her seven sisters were born in Corner Brook where they got used to running water, sidewalks, electricity and the constant smell of sulfur from the mill. But you could tell that the Cove was in Kate's soul. She came off that ferry every June looking pasty, thin and tired. It didn't take more than a couple of days before the fresh sea winds blew away the fausty cobwebs and Kate started behaving like an almost normal teenager. I have to say "almost" because she had her nose in too many books with classy-sounding names to be completely normal. She never read *Teen Confessions* so she knew nothing about the important stuff.

Kate was one of those people who looked ahead and saw what was down the road. She didn't need signs to tell her there were dangerous curves ahead. Me, I needed people yelling at me from all sides before I got a little hint that something could be wrong. My mom liked me to hang out with Kate.

She was the baby in her family and in the Derby clan, the runt of the litter. You might think Kate knew how to take orders, being the tail end of a bossy tribe. No siree! My cousin looked meek and mild hidden behind her hair and glasses but, Lord dyin', she didn't listen to no one. She had her own drum and her own marching tune.

"I don't want no guys sniffing around me," was what she'd been saying for the two summers since her breasts budded out and she became fair dating game in the Cove.

"Boys are only after one thing, and they're not getting it

from me. I'm going to graduate high school." I could hear the steel lock clamp on her cold young heart.

Couldn't blame her. Her sisters were all married and her mom made it clear every chance she got that she didn't want any old maids lolling about. (If you're still hanging around the kitchen when you're eighteen around here, it's a family disgrace.) Susie traipsed down the aisle last summer at seventeen and had a seven-months baby in January. Susie was truly the brilliant one. She could figure out the maths problems faster than the teachers and played the piano like I heard it done on the CBC. Her man had a job in the pulp room at the mill so Susie got a good catch. So her mother said.

It may be a little hard to believe, but we were never really wild. The chores mostly got a lick and a promise and we were off rowing with all our might across the harbor, often for a bare-assed swim but only for a few minutes because the water froze your behind and the mosquitoes and black flies ate you alive and then came back for your last fart. Apart from a little skinny-dipping, a Doris Day movie on Saturday night, reading *Teen Confessions* with a flashlight, and me kissing my Matt endlessly, we didn't do anything too foolish. In past summers we mostly got our kicks picking a whole gallon of blueberries, scooping buckets of mussels, riding the wild horses, exploring in our cave, spreading harmless gossip and, on really hot days, jumping into the sea from the hoist down at the fish plant. Innocents, eh!

The first inkling of real trouble was when that man came to the Cook's Cove annual garden party and time. But, of course we didn't know it then.

CHAPTER TWO

❧

A single line may have two hooks

Whenever Mom said I had to cool my heels I did a little knitting. She knew me inside out and she was on my back about respect for my elders (the gossips were a pain in the arse), tardiness (my Matt and me sometimes lost track of the time) and taking the Lord's name in vain (she would let "Lord jumpin' dyin'" pass and that was about it). She didn't know about the smoking or the home brew. Nevertheless, I got a lot of scarves, mittens and spun-yarn sweaters done last winter.

Rebecca, the perfect daughter, did up scarves and matching caps for the big summer garden party and time all winter. No one had to hold a hot wax candle over her head. She had a schedule written up. Honest to God, I saw it. On Mondays she did green scarves, Tuesdays she knitted blue scarves and on Wednesdays and Thursdays she did the matching caps. Fridays and Saturdays she did up mittens. Sundays she rested but only because the gossips would have ruined her for working on the Lord's Day. Then the week before the garden party she made hazelnut and divinity fudge every night. Big cast-iron pots of it. Miss Committee-Queen-in-Waiting herself.

All four villages in the harbor joined together for the summer garden party and time. Our reputations and community standing as the big family in the Cove depended on us having the best sewing, knitting, rag rugs and crocheting at the sale-of-work, the best baking in the fancy goods stall, and the best dresses at the dance. All the money raised went to the one church built for all the people in the harbor, St. James' Anglican. Folks came in a good mood with lots of change jangling in their pockets. The garden party was in the school front yard during the afternoon and the time, like in having a good time, was the dance in the school hall.

The day before the garden party and time our teacher Miss Hickey suggested Rebecca set up a stall and do sketches for fifty cents apiece. My cousin could watch a person for a minute or two, squiggle a few lines on a page and bingo, there that person was, foibles and all. She had been drawing Kate and me for years and we hardly took any notice except to light the stove with the bits of paper. Miss Hickey caught her doodling in school and Lord dyin', before a tom cod could do a flip, they were calling her an *artist*. Aunt Grace wouldn't have been too happy about Rebecca drawing, wasting her time on nonsense, but she was so tied up organizing the whole she-bang that no one thought to ask her. That's what her committee meeting was about the day Kate arrived. The ladies were going on about twenty-pound turkeys, potato-and-beet salads, dinner rolls and lemon meringue and raspberry pies.

Us Derbys always had the busiest stall at the garden party and this summer wasn't any different. It was called the Derby stall though Mom wasn't technically a Derby. By marrying her cousin, Aunt Grace kept the name. But my mom married into a family from Brittany that settled in the next cove over a hundred years ago. We went by the name of Garreaux though everyone knew we were Derbys. Great-Great-Granddad Derby was the first big independent fish merchant on the west coast of Newfoundland. My great-granddad started up the fish plant where Mom worked. Granddad Derby owned the biggest fleet of boats in the Bay of Islands but he died mortgaged to the hilt. That's another story.

It was true we hadn't seen any real money for a few years but we were still the Derbys. I figured that when I married my Matt I'd technically be a Lewis but of course I'd be a Derby. Went without saying.

Back in time the men on Daddy's side of the family were all fishermen with strong backs, music in their souls and kindly hearts. They were known to give away the fish right out of their nets, to play the fiddle until well past dawn and to charm lobsters into their traps. My daddy didn't mind lending me his dory for a little fun or putting cakes and candy on credit for picnics. He gave me my first draw on a cigarette when I was seven. I was in charge of bringing him his beer and lots of times I helped him put down the brew. He gave me my first sips when Mom wasn't looking. He liked to play the mouth organ and the fiddle and give a good time. He was an only son of an only son and my little brother Georgie would be the one to carry on the family name. Daddy had no qualms about teaching a girl all about boats. He had promised that once I knew all about curing the fish, he would take me out with him as crew. Often I would sit and listen to him play his music at the end of the day, standing near his shoulder. The day he was late coming home, I was the first one to notice.

Along with a basket of knitting, Mom did up a half-dozen cushions crocheted in rainbow squares. Nan worked three of her hooked rugs that were famous around the Bay for their seafaring figures. She drew the fishermen and dories on paper and followed the pattern with her eye and hands. Aunt Grace did up jams and jellies in eye-catching jars with scraps of gingham, ribbons and lace. Kate had a real talent for whittling and she made a dozen old fishermen, cod jiggers and all.

Kate took account of it all and said, "Our best year yet."

There'd been a cold hard rain every day until the Saturday of the garden party. The summer wind scurried over the mountains that backed onto the Cove, picked up speed over the water and whipped at the gables of the saltboxes and Cape Cods. Just when I was planning to wear my long johns to the time, the wind that was nothing but a pain in the butt all week blew away the grayness. A thin northern sunshine brought out the daisies and cotton print dresses mail-ordered out of the spring catalogue and meant for a climate other than our blustery, cool summers.

Me and Kate handled the Derby stall. Rebecca set up a few feet from us. For good luck I noticed she was wearing the beaten gold ring she found washed up on the beach last fall. It was too small for any of her fingers so she had it on a piece of string around her neck. I could see it peeking out a button gap whenever she bent over. I made a mental note to talk to her about going up to the next dress size.

Our stall was the hot spot it was every year. We took in the money hand over fist. In between flirting with the bachelors and the married men alike, I kept an eye on Rebecca and saw to it that she had a mug of nice boiled tea and a plate of molasses cookies on the go. She had a steady stream of dolled-up children with their mothers wiping jam and chocolate cake from their noses and mouths. Rebecca's drawings were not detailed, just a dozen or so pencil strokes, but I saw a lot of smiling mamas holding onto rolled paper the way you'd hold china wrapped in tissue. My mom even had the twins waiting a turn.

We were down to our last pairs of fancy argyle socks when I noticed a stranger standing behind Rebecca watching her sketch. It was odd that I hadn't seen him earlier. No one had told me a strange man was at the garden party. People do come from away for the big day, but they were set up in spare rooms days ago. We'd even figured out how much they would likely spend, depending on if they were relatives from Corner Brook or relatives who were visiting from the mainland. The only way to get into our harbor was by boat, and everyone off the ferry was accounted for. There would be a road in the fall, courtesy of the government, but until that happened, people just didn't drop in from nowhere.

This man was hunched over behind Rebecca holding his hands behind his back. He was frowning. He had narrow eyes and a tight mouth and was quiet as a mouse. He was wearing gray flannels with sharp creases and a navy blazer with shiny buttons.

He sensed me watching him and gave me a hard look. I stared back just as hard. He lowered his eyes, shook himself out, and walked into the school.

Kate was watching him too.

"Have you ever seen him before?" I asked her.

"No," she said, "but that explains why I saw all the children running down to the government wharf about an hour ago. Must have come in on a private yacht."

That did happen from time to time. I mean a fancy yacht finding its way into our harbor, needing fuel or repairs or provisions. Usually it was people from the States out exploring our wild coastline or come to see how the locals lived without flush toilets and electricity. Some of them were surprised to find out we were not Eskimos or heathens.

I had to give up thinking about the stranger because our last customers needed some attention and then it was time to help take down the stalls and do last-minute decorating in the hall. We'd made a couple of hundred roses out of tissue paper in combinations of pink and white and they all had to be strung across the ceiling.

We made a whack of money for the church and handed it over to the Ladies' Aid committee just busting with pride. Aunt Grace had disappeared and so had the stranger. I wanted to dash down to the wharf to see what kind of yacht was tied up but there just wasn't a moment. I had to run all the way Upalong, dragging Kate behind me to get ready for the time.

I loosened and unclipped the pin curls I'd been hiding all day under a flowered bandana. My copper hair had lots of bounce but for the dance I teased it high into a beehive with a half dozen ringlets falling down the back. My dress was brand-new. It had come on the boat in Friday's mail.

No sleeve bouffant dress. Very swish, very much the big occasion, for after dark. The gleam and rustle of its gala fabric suggests a party mood wherever it goes. Chromspun Rayon Taffeta, scalloped neckline dips gracefully lower in the back, draped cummerbund effect, all-'round the waist accents the slim-fitting bodice flatteringly—in the back a great big fishtail bow. Sapphire blue. $14.98

Wasn't I the cat's meow! Smoothing down the front in the mirror and straightening the bow, I told myself here was one gal with some natural curves who could wear bouffant. I took a deep breath and felt I was ready to help Kate.

The wind and rain all week meant Kate could read and get bad ideas. Like announcing, on the Monday before, that she wasn't going to no time this summer.

"I'm not in the marriage market and that time is nothing but a coming-out party," said my dear cousin. She'd been reading too many Jane Austens.

I wasn't about to let her get off with not dancing the night away with every old goat and bum pincher in the Cove. A Derby had her duty, especially one carrying the name. That's when I remembered that she and Chas might make a good couple.

My Matt came by on Wednesday to get help with the children's fishpond Aunt Grace had told him to set up. I was baking pies and up to my neck in pastry. Kate couldn't find my new hiding place for her book so was tormenting me by eating the raspberries. She offered to help my Matt and before the words were out of her mouth, Chas came in with boxes of balloons, kewpie dolls and paper airplanes from his dad's general store. My Matt had more collecting to do, so my cousin helped Chas.

It wasn't too big a sacrifice. From the kitchen I heard them jabbering like magpies about the new road that meant we could stay put and not be obliged to move like people in many other isolated outports had to, and about Captain Cook, the great explorer who charted our coast and gave us his name. They were both a bit weird. That's when I figured they just might be meant for each other.

As the light faded I sent Nan into the dining room with the oil lamp and a plate of fresh raspberry tarts. Chas, always a cool dude, said he had to be getting on home but that he wanted to hear more of what Kate had to say about Newfoundland politics and that he would come by with Matt on Saturday evening. Pretty smooth. He was gone a full five minutes before Kate let out a howl, picked up the broom and chased me around the kitchen, saying she had been tricked into a date for the time.

I let her eat my share of the tarts while I told her what I would do with her pink dress.

And now it was Saturday. The dress looked a lot better after

I took out the crinoline and put in a couple of deep darts. Kate even managed to sit still while I combed out her tatty hair. A hundred brush-strokes later it was shining and golden and I could just begin to see that she had possibilities. But wouldn't you know it, she grabbed the whole blond mass of it and tied it back with an old rubber band. I did manage to tease her bangs a little and dab a bit of lipstick on her mouth.

Kate got to her feet and we started down the front stairs, me with a flourish and a swish of my crinoline, 'cause the boys were watching. Kate slunk down behind me. Mom and Nan made a big deal over how great we looked. I lapped it up. My Matt's eyes said something like "luscious."

But, you know, Chas didn't notice a thing. He just carried on the talk they were having earlier in the week. "The road will change everything. The government had no right to bring in a resettlement program just so it could cut out the medical boats." You could tell he'd been saving it up for days. Like I said, weird.

I was planning to make a big entrance at the school. But in the end we had to wear rubber boots because of the rain all week, me carrying my two-and-three-quarter-inch stiletto heels and Kate her court shoes in paper bags. At the last minute Mom asked us to take the twins 'cause she and Nan still needed to take out pin curls and pack on the old rouge. So picture this. Instead of the grand debut due a daughter of the Derby house, there I was in black rubber boots with red soles reeking of fish offal, practically dragging two kids across the fields and dodging sheep and jumping potato rows, 'cause we were late and through the fields was the quickest way to the school.

Never mind. My toes started tapping as soon as I heard the piano accordion squealing out "The Kelligrew's Soiree." Rebecca was on the dance floor wearing a shiny purple dress almost the same color as the lilacs in her hair. I grabbed my Matt for a fast round and was into the duty dances quick as a wink. The manager of the fish plant danced like a turkey and I had trouble hanging on and keeping up. The fiddlers were going faster than Don Messer and the Islanders. I was gasping for breath when the school principal took my hand and we did a rip-roaring reel to "I'se the B'y."

"Save me, Matt darlin'," I cried. But he was into the beer with the boys and clapped for more action louder than anyone.

While I whirled with a couple of the old Cove bachelors I noticed that Kate was missing and that the stranger I'd seen that afternoon was talking to Aunt Grace. I had to find out what was going on. But my aunt's body was turned away from me. Her head was bent into the circle she and the stranger had created. Her shoulders were hunched forward and her face was taut, her eyes hooded.

It looked like he wasn't in a good mood. First of all he wasn't drinking anything, his hands were in his pants pockets, his tie was too straight, his hair too stiff. He was talking to my aunt but he wasn't looking at her. He was talking over her shoulder, not meeting her eyes. His body was still, just the air being pressed in and out of his full cheeks.

They were much the same age, both with a touch of gray, much the same height, he carrying more weight. They were talking like they were in a bubble, like the dancers swirling around them didn't exist, like they didn't hear the music. Like they were in another time and place. A good thirty seconds evaporated while I lounged in the shadows against the wall. Then Aunt Grace made an abrupt movement and the chat was over.

She walked into the school kitchen. In a few minutes the stranger headed toward my mother. I made a beeline for her too.

"Hello, Mrs. Garreaux. My name is Franklin Harris. Your neighbors just pointed you out to me. I'm pleased to meet you. And this, I understand, is your daughter, Melinda. I'm very pleased to meet you, Melinda. I believe I saw you this afternoon," he said, as charmingly as any Victorian gentleman.

We stood there with our mouths hanging open. Finally I got up enough nerve to say that we were pleased to meet him. My mom had never been very brave with outsiders, so I figured it was up to me to fill in the gaps.

"We hope you're enjoying the time, Mr. Harris. How did you get here?"

This was a bit rough but it was the first thing that popped into my head and out of my mouth it came. And bless his soul but he took the bait and told us all about his yacht and his plans to see something different every summer and his interest in Newfoundland because he'd met so many Newfoundlanders in his bank in Boston. Good people, he said. Hard workers. He told us there was a nice cabin on his boat so he didn't need hotels and that he had a hired man to take care of the cooking and the repairs, that he'd seen some rough water around Newfoundland and was glad he had good charts. He was as pleasant as could be and full of the everyday talk that finally put my mother at ease.

Then he got to his point. It sounded so casual, as he said to my mother, "I was asking your sister about her daughter. I saw the girl drawing this afternoon at the garden party and I thought she was very good. Has she had any training?"

"Well, no," Mom said. "She has dozens of books on art that she reads over and over but there's nowhere to get training around here. She's always liked to use pencils and I guess has been good at making pictures of fish and birds since she was a very little girl. She was born in Halifax and spent her early years there and when the family came back here, she had a box of pencils with her. We thought it was very cute. She's had pencil and paper with her ever since."

Did Mr. Harris raise a slight eyebrow when my mother said Halifax?

"I like her work," he said, "and my bank is involved with an art college in Boston. I was asking your sister about letting Rebecca come to Boston to train at the college for a couple of weeks later this summer. The college has a wonderful program for young people. I can arrange for her to stay with my sister and her family. The bank has a special fund to help young artists and would pay her airfare and fees. But your sister is very opposed to the idea. I'm wondering if perhaps the problem is that she wouldn't want Rebecca to go alone. That's why I sought you out, Mrs. Garreaux. Perhaps your daughter here would like to accompany her cousin to Boston. My sister has a big house and would enjoy hosting both young ladies. Of course we would pay all Melinda's costs too. And I can give you character references for myself and my sister. We're well known in Boston."

My mother didn't know where to turn. Her face flushed, her hands clenched in a bony knot. She wouldn't look at me so she couldn't see my eyes saying yes. She drew a couple of quick breaths and gave him the only answer she could.

"That's a very kind offer, Mr. Harris, and it is lovely that you see some talent in our Rebecca, but if her mother is against it, there's nothing else to be said. Grace is head of the family and what she says goes."

He said he was surprised we could just let Rebecca's talent go to waste, that he wanted to help, that it wasn't every day he saw someone as gifted as my cousin, that it was a shame not to give her a chance, and could my mother at least ask her sister to think about it one more time?

By this time my mother was getting flustered as she tried to say no but remain polite.

My mom had always looked up to her older sister. Grace took charge and was big enough to be seen and heard. My mom was like a fuzzy black-and-white photo. The two sisters walked into a room and a light shone from Grace, her blondness a halo and the ice blue of her eyes catching the reflected light. My mom disappeared into Grace's shine and shadow. Her hair had always been brown and by last summer it was a speckled starling color. She was happiest slinking off to a corner and melting into the wallpaper. 'Course, that was only when she was with her sister. When she put her foot down in our kitchen, the floor shook and we paid heed, at least for a little while.

Mr. Harris just wouldn't take no for an answer. Maybe he saw the gleam of want that shot into my eyes at the thought of two weeks in Boston. In the end my mom mumbled something about seeing what she could do and left Mr. Harris watching the dancing to find Nan to make sure she had her tea and a bite to eat.

I found Kate out back in a big argument with Chas over Confederation. I guess you could say it was a semi-formal debate because each was being egged on by a jumble of men. The sparring was mostly good-natured but the jabs were clear. This was a grown-up man's sport. But Kate knew her politics, and you could see that to these guys her hair and cat's-eye spectacles didn't matter.

I broke through the crowd. The smoke tickled my throat and almost made me dizzy with want.

"The fishery has been in trouble before and it's always come back. It's back now and Joey Smallwood had nothing to do with it. We needed more jobs, not a new country. We pay too high a price for welfare checks in the mail. We should have thought harder about the offer from the U.S. We need fewer handouts and more work," argued our Kate.

I saw my chance to jump in. "Holy Lord dyin'. I bring Kate to a dance and look where she ends up. Stop your yakking, Mr. Park. I needs to talk to Kate right now. Let me through. Come on, my maid, you must be lockjawed by now."

It didn't take me long to fill Kate in on the details. We dragged Rebecca off the dance floor and into a dark corner and told her all about Mr. Harris. She came right out and said that going to art school was a dream so sacred she never even told us about it.

We knew where she stood. Now we had to make it happen.

First we had to get through this evening and show the crowd a good time. The music was still thumping, the time must go on. I even pushed Kate onto the dance floor and she did a funny twisty thing that she heard about on a radio station from the States. Lordy, it caught on, and before the next reel was called my Matt and Chas took up the fiddle and spoons, caught the rhythm, and the young ones were on the floor jiggling up a storm.

I wasn't having too much fun to notice that Aunt Grace was in the shadows against the wall chatting up Robert Gordon. He was listening to my aunt, but his eyes were following Rebecca around the dance floor. He was a bachelor in his late thirties whose mother died in the spring and for the first time he was living on his own. Trouble.

Another reason to get Rebecca to Boston.

CHAPTER THREE

❧

Tinker, tailor,
Soldier, sailor,
Rich man, poor man,
Beggarman, thief

I knew as soon as we stepped into the aisle after church the next day that there was a buzz about Rebecca and the stranger. Someone had made up the story that the man was rich and he wanted Rebecca to go to Boston to do sketches of his children. By the time we bid our goodbyes at the church gate, I had picked up the whispers that the Lady of Down Below was pretty upset, and that Rebecca wasn't going nowhere.

Well.

Me and Kate dallied along home. She said something about Chas asking her out again but I didn't catch it because Rebecca was on my mind. By the time we were along our lane, Nan and Mom had their stockings and hats off and were in the kitchen with fancy aprons over their best cotton dresses. Georgie and Flossie were going wild out back along the brook, catching minnows and cutting off their tails. There was a heat mist coming off the harbor and it was hot in the kitchen with the Mitchell stove stoked up for the regular

Sunday dinner of boiled potatoes, turnip, cabbage, salt beef and figgy duff. The CBC was on the radio and the hymns were enough to make you want to repent all your sins.

The air was heavy with sweet lilac perfume. The front of our house was practically covered in bushes reaching up to the second story. My great-granddad planted them in the rocky soil and they took on the sheltered side of our windy hill. Kate always said it was the lilacs why she stayed with us when she came for her summer visits. But that was hogwash because Aunt Grace had a lilac bush near her side door. She stayed with us because she liked being pampered by Nan. Aunt Grace had a beautifully done-up guest room, but if Kate were to stay with Aunt Grace she'd have to work her fingers to the bone, act like an Anglican, and be forever serving afternoon tea to one of my aunt's women's committees. At our house she stayed in my room on a lumpy foldout bed, but she liked it that way. She was strange about liking the old family house with all its add-ons and nooks. Of course she was never there in the winter, when the upstairs was so cold that damp towels froze solid hanging on the washstands. After October, me, Nan, Mom and the twins all set up beds in the dining room and kept the kitchen door open to get the heat from the woodstove. My mom was saving her money to buy an oil-heater for the upstairs. She'd been saving for two or three years and was so close she was looking at them in the catalogue.

"Our lilacs looked real good in church," I said to my mother, trying to butter her up. I offered to take the twins down to the beach for a proper swim after dinner.

"That would be grand. I need a rest after all the overtime this week. I hates to see a heavy run on the herring. My poor bones can't take it anymore but we need the money. There's a silver lining to every cloud."

That was about the only complaint we ever heard from my mother. She'd been raised to a hard life and had been a fisherman's wife but she never went on about the bad times. I could see the deep lines forming in her forehead, the touch of gray in her hair, the cuts on her hands, the rough skin on her neck and her red-rimmed eyes. Nan did the housework and got the meals started but our mom was, well, our mom, and she had us all swarming after her every minute she was in the house. No matter how tired she was she'd sit with her black coffee, her hand-rolled cigarettes, a pack of cards for solitaire, her long skinny legs resting on a stool and listen and do her best to sort us out.

I began to lay the table for dinner. Mom liked to have it look nice on Sunday. She always said that if her sister could put a white cloth on the table every day, then the least we could do was to have one on Sunday.

The Battenberg lace cloth was washed but wrinkled. The iron was hot on the stove and I tested it with a stab of my wet finger. I loved to see the big white cloth tamed by the hot iron.

"Aye, you'll run a fine home someday, Melinda, my darlin'," said my mom.

With a grand opening like that, I couldn't help but jump right in.

"My Matt wants us to get married as soon as he lays up his boat this fall," I said as I brought the cloth to the table.

She put down the pan of potatoes and stuck her fingers in her ears.

"I don't want to hear another thing about a wedding. I told you, you have to finish high school. You're the smartest girl there ever was in the Cove, probably the whole harbor, and you're not wasting your brains, do you hear me?" she asked, almost raising her voice.

I had her good and riled. I smoothed the cloth, put the cut-glass sugar basin and blue milk jug on the table, turned ever so slowly for effect, and went at her while she was tired and hungry. The things a girl had to do.

"Maybe we could come up with something that will keep us both happy," I said.

She was suspicious but interested.

"I'm thinking that if you talk Aunt Grace into letting Rebecca go to Boston, and I can go with her like that Mr. Harris suggested, I'll stay in school, finish up and marry my Matt next summer," I said.

Her mind was racing. She even stopped pouring the water off the potatoes.

"It's a good plan, maid, but Grace is dead set against Rebecca going to Boston and you're old enough to know what your aunt is like," she said.

There was no doubt I knew my aunt. Since I could remember she'd been a second mother to me. My mom would spoil me with jam tarts and hugs. Aunt Grace would teach me my prayers, check my homework and think nothing of slapping my knuckles if I hit the wrong key while practicing the piano. It's been that way since my dad died, maybe even before.

I'd been told that I looked more like my Aunt Grace than my mom, even though Grace was blond and I was a redhead. We were the same solid build, both of us as tall as most of the men around here. We had the same blue eyes and the same sculpted cheeks. I had a narrow waist, curvy hips and a high, full bosom. You could see that Aunt Grace had them too, not so long ago. Some folks said that I was as bossy as my aunt. But if it was true, we were bossy in different ways. Aunt Grace put all her energy into raising a perfect Christian daughter and squeezing every penny out of us sinners to pay for the latest repairs up at the church. If I meddled, I liked to think it was to help someone out of a fix.

Like the one Rebecca was in. I figured I would show my mom the biggest trump card I had.

"Remember your dream about me becoming a nurse? Maybe if I went to Boston I could look into nursing for after high school," I said, and slid into the pantry to help Nan with the pudding.

I was torn about studying to be a nurse. I'd always liked visiting the sick with Aunt Grace, and people said I had the healing hands just like my aunt. I could tell when a fever was going to break, where a broken bone needed to be set, how to sew up a deep cut. I loved stopping the pain. But I loved my Matt too and I knew he wanted so bad to get married, finish the house, have children. I did think that if I could get away for a couple of weeks, it would be a kind of test. If I survived for two weeks away from the Cove and my Matt, maybe I would last the two years of nursing school. So I wasn't just baiting my mom.

I watched her through the doorway. Her eyes grew bigger than the plates she was carrying to the table. Her cigarette went unlit and dangled from the corner of her mouth. For a moment or two her hands were extended over the table with a couple of plates in mid-air.

She turned and came into the pantry.

"What about your Matt? Will he let you go?" she asked.

When he walked me home from the time the night before my head was buzzing with Boston. The idea of looking into the nursing schools hadn't just popped into my head while talking to my mom. It had come to me the night before just as my Matt started nibbling my ear out on the back porch. Usually when he nibbled, it was just the beginning of a cozy necking session. But his look told me he knew my mind wasn't on loving him. So I spread out all the pros and cons of me going to Boston and being a nurse and in the end, he simply took me in his big arms and said that whatever I wanted to do was all right with him. I cried. What else could I do when a man who wants nothing more than to have a wife says he'll wait three years.

I shouldn't have been surprised. He had been waiting for me to grow up the past couple of years and had been gentle and kind forever. He knew about my sick visits and how folks kept saying I should be a proper nurse.

My Matt was a fisherman's son and his dream was to have a snug boat and a wife to come home to. He was seven years older than me and he should have been married by now but our hearts have been bound together ever since my dad and his little brother died within a month of one another. My dad went overboard when he was out fishing. Matt's brother, Luke, died on the water too, but in a little boat that was trying to get him to the hospital in the city on a bitter day in December. It turned out he had a bad appendix and it burst before the rescue boat was halfway up the Bay. Luke had been in my grade at school. The way my Matt told the story was that he was so lonely when Luke died that he thought he was going to die of a broken heart himself.

Then over breakfast one morning his mom saw me passing their window, a ten-year-old waif who had just lost her daddy, and she said that little girl could sure use a friend. In February my Matt started coming around to help me with my homework, to help Mom with the twins and the woodpile and to cheer us up with his fiddle music. We grew to be best buddies and then one night, after I turned thirteen, it struck me like a snowball between the eyes. I loved my friend. He dragged it out of me because, he said, I was acting real strange and he admitted that he had truly loved me for at least six months and that he had been working real hard at being patient about me growing up.

My Matt was a good man. He let me do the talking but I always searched his eyes for his approval. A slight frown tucked between his bushy brows meant I'd gone too far. His mouth tightened at the corners when he was warning me not to get cross with my mom or my nan.

My Matt worked hard for his living. He was in the boat with his father well before dawn and when he was not fishing he was readying fresh bait and fixing lines, nets and traps. From April to October none of the fishermen slept much more than five hours a night. Sometimes they caught a nap in the boat while heading home from the fishing grounds. The fishing started in the springtime with the run on the herring, then there was the cod and the halibut and in between was the lobster and salmon fishery and the caplin they needed for bait, and then the herring again in the fall. In the winter he worked in the woods, hauling logs for the paper mill in Corner Brook.

I hardly saw my Matt most of the summer, often just on Sundays. That was why he wanted so bad to get married. He was just too tired to come over for a visit or go for a walk and when he could it was usually so late he wouldn't dare because Nan would likely chase him with a chunk of wood. And my Matt and his dad went to their summer fishing camp for five or six weeks right after the time. But he had never been able to refuse me anything, so I told Mom not to worry about him. She said she would think about it some more.

Folks here said the three of us cousins were good together. Without Rebecca and Kate, I might have been bored enough to sneak over to my Matt's summer camp and do dangerous and delightful things down behind his fish shack. Without me, Rebecca would have been wedged under her mom's thumb, and without me and Rebecca, Kate would have starved to death.

All this commotion meant it was time for girl talk.

The next day, Monday, happened to be a beaut of a day. The kind you had to snatch from the kitchen gods, else you wouldn't remember we had a summer. The sun was warm, the wind had found another cove to harass and the water was dead calm. We wrapped salt beef in greaseproof paper, buttered big chunks of bread, stole some hermits from the cookie jar, filled up a bottle with orange Freshie and took a dipper and bucket to make us look like honest working girls going berry-picking. The twins noticed real quick that we were up to something and ran to find their swim gear. Kate buttered more bread and we all set off down the lane to find Rebecca.

The kitchen Down Below was deserted. After shouting up the stairs and around the hall into the parlor we figured there was no one home and we headed over to the fish stage. She was there all right, chopping off heads and splitting cod and halibut. She was strong, fast and precise. I never tired of seeing the graceful sweep of a hand slitting the cod's throat, taking the cut down through the belly to the tail, breaking off the head, taking out the stomach and, with another single movement, spreading the fish wide, ready for drying.

Uncle Wilf saw us over Rebecca's shoulder. "Go on, my love. Go with your cousins and have some fun. Don't get into trouble, mind that Melinda," he said. He knew I heard him and I flashed him a grin. He was always kidding around.

"Can we take your rowboat?" I asked.

Uncle Wilf took a draw on his soggy cigarette, nodded his dark shaggy curls. He never said no. I was pretty sure he didn't know the word.

We were off running to the end of the stage where the Derbys had tied up their boats for a hundred years or more.

My daddy's boat was there and Uncle Wilf always kept it in good repair. We could have gone across the harbor faster in our dory with the outboard engine but the day was so still a motor would have been a sin. Besides, I was never allowed to take Dad's boat unless my mom said so and I always had to tell her where I was going.

Rebecca grabbed an oar, I latched onto the other one and Kate and the twins cuddled up in the bow with the picnic and the berry bucket. Not one word was spoken but we all knew where we were going.

Twenty minutes later Kate was hollering for us to mind the rocks as we pushed ashore. The rotting foundation of the house where my nan grew up was in front of us and the pinks, blues and greens of Cook's Cove houses dotted the land behind us. The church steeple was clear on the hill and so were the white headstones spread in neat rows in the cemetery. The people and sounds were out of range, silent as the graves.

I splashed into the icy sea, felt the kelp between my toes and tried for a hold on the slimy, snail-encrusted boulders. While I held the boat away from the jagged rocks, Rebecca reached for a deeply rooted birch sapling that bent toward the water and she tied our line to it. We carried the twins ashore. You don't know cold until you go cold turkey into the North Atlantic, even in July. We were in and out faster than crabs.

We hit the meadow at a run, our skirts swishing in the tall grass and catching on the thistle thorns. Lilies of the valley hid in the marshy spots, but their delicate sweet scent gave them away. Kate sent the twins to search out a bouquet. Georgie got the job of flicking off the ants. Robins were hopping about and screeching sea gulls were brazenly eyeing our lunch basket.

This sea of wild grass was called the Neck, and was just a

pathway for us between the shoreline where we tied up the rowboat and another beach tucked away on the sheltered side of Cook's Point, a rocky land mass that jutted like a finger out into the Bay.

The rocks that made up the Point had a split personality. On the side where we landed, the cliffs were gray and heartless, but once through the Neck and on the other side of Cook's Point, the rock itself was a shelter from the Atlantic winds. Pine, spruce and fir trees grew thin, but straight and tall. Springy moss filled in where the trees couldn't drop anchor. Best of all, just where the rock started its sharp descent to the bottom of the sea, there was a deep split in the cliff. That was where we were headed. Our old pirate cave, lapped by the calm waters of a tiny cove.

We walked along the stony beach, breathed in the briny air and listened to the screaming gulls. Every few steps one of us picked up a flat rock and skimmed it across the water. Rebecca had the best hand for this and could gracefully skip a smooth stone four or five times. We jacked up our skirts and splashed knee-deep into the cold water. After a few seconds the water felt almost warm enough for a swim. But we were not quite that stunned. We knew we would freeze in an instant.

It was clear that no one had been out to the cave since our last visit. We'd left a pile of kindling and rocks on a ledge about ten feet from the opening with a box of matches wrapped in tarpaper, ready for a fire. It was one of our games, leaving the cave ready for a shipwrecked sailor or fisherman, or pirate.

The cave, shaped like an Indian teepee, had weathered at least one bad storm since last fall. A boulder close to the entrance that we had used as a picnic table was split down the middle. Rocks as big as Sunday cabbages had been tossed from the sea and filled a hole we'd used as a hiding place when we were little.

The rocky ledge in front of the cave caught the sun. That's where we settled, on the warm spots on the flat black rocks. We lay belly down and yanked up our skirts some more. I took out the pack of Export As I'd hidden in the picnic and set out four on the rock. My quota for the day. Both cousins groaned. I took no heed but warned the kiddies with a hard look not to tell. From this perch we could watch the tide. The twins were quickly undressed and in their bathing suits, splashing in the water where we could see them but they couldn't hear us.

We started with our old game of counting buttons. Somehow I always ended up with four. That day it was four down the front of my blouse and one missing from my skirt waistband. There was little doubt I'd be marrying a sailor, the same thing as a fisherman. Rebecca and Kate each had enough sense to keep their buttons sewn on, so they came up with five each. That meant a rich man. Which reminded me.

"So," I said, "Kate, what were you trying to tell me the other day about you and Chas?" A blush started at her collarbone, but this was where we bared our souls so there was no holding back.

"Well, it's just that I think he's nice," she said.

Our Kate was smitten. For her to say a boy was nice was pretty serious stuff. Me and Rebecca let the gentle waves fill the silence. I practiced exhaling smoke through my nostrils the way the boys did when they were showing off.

"He reads all the time, and he listens," she said while she got redder and redder.

"Mmmmmmmm," was all I said at first. Then I pushed my shoulders back, squinted into the sun and jumped in with the only question worth asking.

"Has he kissed you yet?" She hid behind her bangs but nodded.

I couldn't believe it. My scrawny cousin was starting a big romance right under my nose and I hadn't seen it. I could tell from the queer smile on her crimson face that she liked that kiss.

She was such a bookworm and so out of the in-crowd stuff she didn't even realize that Chas was the number-one catch in the Cove. His family was the agent for the big fish buyers and owned the contract for supplying everything we needed in the harbor from safety pins to fish netting. Chas only had one sister, who was already married, and he would come into a good business. Nice body, too, and even cuter than my Matt—the James Dean look without the anger. He was especially in demand because he drove the only vehicle in the Cove. It was a Ford truck, mostly used for the store, but Chas could get it any time to drive the five miles of road around the harbor.

I wondered if I should tell her that his girlfriends lasted about one month. Nah, I decided, she'd find out. None of my business.

"Hey, Rebecca," I said. "Let me see that ring again."

She pulled the string up from the inside of her blouse, untied the knot and handed me the little band of gold. It was tiny and rough with a pure white stone. Rebecca found it washed up in this cove. She swore it gave her good luck. She wore it this year for the provincial exams. I wondered if she would beat me. I'd been leaving her in the dust for all her sweating over the books.

"You'd better give that ring a few good rubs if you want to go to Boston," I said. That was enough to get us going.

"I don't understand," said Rebecca. "Mom used to come around to anything I really wanted. She's tough but she usually gives in if it's important to me. She won't budge this time. Not an inch. She sets her jaw and a hardness comes into her eyes. She won't even talk about it. Dad's no good up against Mom. Don't you think it's a bit strange? Mom spent two years in Boston during the war. I thought she'd want me to see it. She won't even listen when I tell her that you will come with me. Do you get the feeling something is going on?"

I lit another cigarette and got to thinking about Aunt Grace. She was from here, she was one of us, but she stood apart. There was even a time when I thought my aunt was a princess come to us from far away. She was always so perfect. I'd flip through the old catalogues looking for cutouts and I'd see her on every page—beautiful blond women in tailored dresses with matching gloves and hats. I asked my mom once how Grace was related to us and how she came to Cook's Cove. Mom laughed, but I was serious. I couldn't figure out how this lady came to live among us.

Even though Grace and Uncle Wilf and Rebecca ate at the kitchen table like everyone else in the Cove, the cloth was always white and crisp, the dishes matched and there were white cloth napkins. The dirty plates were taken to the pantry before dessert was handed around on matching side plates, and Aunt Grace poured the tea out of a teapot into china cups with matching cream jug and sugar bowl. Nobody swished her teabag into a chipped mug at Aunt Grace's.

Funny thing, though. I liked having my supper there whenever I could wangle an invite or arrange to be there just when supper was ready. While we cleaned up the kitchen, Aunt Grace would slip into the parlor and practice the hymns for Sunday. Uncle Wilf smoked on the daybed and Rebecca and me tidied up without a word. It was the life we would have had if my dad had lived. Since he drowned, my mom didn't have the energy for pretty china and the fancy chocolate eclairs and jelly rolls Aunt Grace was famous for in the Cove.

Aunt or no aunt, I was bursting to help my cousin. We'd been through too much together for me to let her down now. We were practically sisters, with two mothers and one father shared between us. She knew where my mug was kept in our pantry and I knew where she hid the sheet music Aunt Grace didn't want us to play.

"Look," I said. "We're going to need some kind of identification and even a vaccination to go across the border. I'm pretty sure that's what Miss Hickey said she had to have when she went to Maine last year. Remember all the fuss about her getting a new birth certificate because the church had burnt down in Bonavista? And she had a new Canadian passport too. Just about all the Derby papers are in the family Bible Upalong but I've never seen your birth certificate there. If we had it maybe we could beg for a trip into the city, and sneak off to the government building and fill out any forms we need to get ourselves ready for Boston."

That was me, jumping in feet first. I was on a roll.

"Aunt Grace has to go over to Beach Cove on Thursday to help the Ladies' Aid organize a church supper. I heard her say she'll overnight with Mrs. Robinson. That's the same night as the Orange Lodge. I say we do a grand search for your birth certificate that night and go into Corner Brook early next week. We'll have it back before your mom knows it's gone. We'll get the smallpox shot and we'll be all ready to go as soon as Aunt Grace gets right in her head," I said.

It worked. Rebecca smiled, her eyes said thank you and finally I could talk about my very favorite subject, my Matt.

"I slipped over to see how the house was coming along yesterday. The studs are up and you can see where the rooms are going to be. There are three bedrooms and an inside outhouse. The kitchen is big and I'll be able to do the wash with the machine hooked up to the sink. My Matt has got it all planned out. We're going to have an electric stove and an electric water pump. My Matt figures we'll get electricity pretty soon after the road comes through in September. I'll just have to turn a dial to get the kettle boiled. And we'll get a television too. My Matt wants us to get married in November. He can't do much more on the house until after the fishing. He's working almost double this summer and is putting every extra penny into saving for the house. A part of me wants to get married too, desperately. I'd be a married lady with my own house. Then I think maybe another year in school isn't so bad and maybe even nursing training and Mom would be so happy. Who do I please, my Matt or Mom?"

My cousins wouldn't answer because I had asked that same question too many times already. They always said I should do what made me the happiest. Lord dyin', how was a girl supposed to know what made her happy until she did it?

We watched the tide come in, yoo-hooed to the twins and reached for the food. We were so hungry we scoffed it down and wiped off our fingers in a little tidal pool that smelled of crabs and snails.

There was something else I needed to know from Rebecca, and I'd never known how to stop my tongue. Out it came. "Didn't I see you walk home with Robert Gordon after the time?" I asked her.

"We left the school together and walked Down Below because Mom asked Robert to carry some bowls. I can still give you a licking if you're suggesting for one minute that old geezer walked me home. Besides, if you want to know, he didn't say one word to me the whole way. Don't go spreading any idle gossip about me and Robert. He's an old man, for God's sake, must be close to forty."

"He's got a nice house," I tried to say, but had trouble finishing the sentence because she was up chasing me and throwing dippers of cold water as she ran.

I called a truce. It was time to pick some raspberries to make honest maidens of us. We scratched our arms and mussed up our hair in the brambles but we had a grand old time talking about lipstick, pedal-pushers and Sunset nail polish, and goosing Kate about our grade ten exams. She wanted so bad to get top marks to get a scholarship to university next year. It was the only way she'd be able to go because her parents certainly didn't believe in girls getting an education.

Under the cover of our chatter, I fretted. I had never crossed my aunt before on anything that mattered. For all my big talk, I was scared. Maybe we were going too far.

CHAPTER FOUR

❧

An open door would tempt a saint

Folks in the Cove lived by the Bible on Sunday and by little bits of wisdom that came from who knows where the rest of the week. *A penny saved is a penny earned, Misfortunes come of themselves, Misfortunes find their way even on the darkest night, A bad penny always turns up, Two wrongs do not make a right, Debt is the worst poverty, and Fortune is made of glass.* You get the picture. No matter, disaster was always around the corner waiting to hit us on the head.

On the Sunday afternoon before our visit to the cave, I had dragged Kate down to the government wharf to see the big yacht Mr. Harris had tied up there. She didn't want to come, because Chas was in charge of provisioning the boat and she was scared he'd think she was checking up on him. I finally convinced her this was silly, but she still held back and hid behind the fish crates anyway.

Mr. Harris was hurrying Chas along because he wanted to leave in time to get clear of the coastline before dark. He had a big smile full of white teeth and his voice was gentle as he spoke to the children hanging around the wharf. He was even giving them red jawbreakers. I hung back but he saw me. It was like he was looking out for me.

"Hello, young lady. Has your aunt changed her mind?" For once I was tongue-tied and could only shake my head. After hesitating a moment, he dug into his pocket and then held out his hand to me.

"Here," he said. "Let me give you my address at the bank. If your aunt changes her mind, she can send me a telegram and I'll set everything up. Keep in mind that the art course starts in August. Your cousin is very talented, you know."

I took the small card and stuffed it in my skirt pocket and mumbled a thank-you and a goodbye, the way I was raised to do. There was a commotion as the last boxes were stowed down the hold and the ropes were slipped for his departure.

The yacht moved away from the wharf. As Mr. Harris raised his sail, he shouted across the wind, "You are your aunt all over again." Kate was over fluttering her eyelashes at Chas and she didn't notice a thing. I couldn't have heard him right.

Thursday dawned with a harsh east wind and a winter chill uncommon even for us for July. Kate was up, dressed in trousers and a heavy pullover. She threw my green-and-white Fair Isle sweater across the bed and asked where I'd hidden the warm socks. I took a look out the window and decided that the water was probably too rough for Aunt Grace to make it over to Beach Cove. Maybe the weather would decide our fate, as it so often did in our lives.

Kate and I headed for a breakfast of fried eggs, bacon, left-over baked beans, and big chunks of bread toasted over the open damper. We were just in time for Nan to beat down the bread dough and she hacked off a heap of it for us. Kate patted the dough into little bits and fried the pieces in the bacon fat. Golden brown toutons. Some good. I took in that Nan was acting pretty normal. She always went a little wacko if a storm was coming. Then Nan told me she was watching out the window and saw Uncle Wilf and Aunt Grace leave for Beach Cove.

Me and Kate worked most of the day indoors taking down grass-green and gold wallpaper from Flossie's new room. It was a mistake even twenty years ago, Nan told us, but it was all that came in on the boat that spring. You could find the same paper in most of the houses in the Cove. The paper had brown blotches where the roof once leaked and it was peeling away near the top. The bedroom hadn't been used for years and years but Flossie announced last winter that now that she was five, she wanted her own Princess Room. The pink-and-white rose pattern from the catalogue would make the room look real clean and bright. Nan was working on a rosy patch-work quilt and was making a dark pink hooked rug. It would be just like that Shirley Temple's room in the movie magazines. We all adored the twin because she was such a cutie-pie, all dimples and smiles, golden-red curls and the Derby blue eyes. Georgie was cute too but he wasn't a girl.

Rebecca dropped by to tell us that Uncle Wilf would be going to the Lodge around seven. She sat on the floor with her sketchpad and did drawing after drawing of us hanging the wallpaper. Then she tossed them all in the stove, like she always did, and left to get her dad his supper.

Nan made a fish stew for us and Kate fried up a stack of yesterday's bread in bacon fat. One of my favorite suppers. There was raspberry grunt for dessert. Kate's plate was empty and I was almost sure she had let her belt out a notch. I stole a glance at Mom's plate. She had pushed it away, hardly eaten, and was using the painted roses around the edge as an ashtray. She spread out the cards for a game of solitaire. Something was worrying her.

They were behind with the smoked herring down at the factory. "The tang of the sea retained in every pair of kippers," said the label on every tin that left the Cove for the States and for Europe. They were starting another shift to catch up and my mom latched on to every scrap of extra work that came along. She looked bone tired with her curved back and smudges around her eyes.

I borrowed the torch from the nook under the stairs and shoved it under my sweater as I passed through the kitchen. We told Mom we were going Down Below to visit with Rebecca but she hardly looked up from her cards. Kate headed down the lane in front of me. We turned our bodies into the cold wind coming in over the water.

Aunt Grace's kitchen was warm but Rebecca was jumpy.

"What took you so long? You said you were coming right after supper. Dad's been gone a half-hour," said my cousin as she barred the door. She wasn't wasting any time.

Kate and I both knew it was pretty saucy of us to go searching in Aunt Grace's house. Sure we were allowed in the parlor, because we were close family. But we knew not to touch anything, especially not to open boxes, cupboards or drawers. My mom would probably cut off my hand if she found out I picked up a photograph or ornament and she'd go after my tongue if she knew I'd been snooping through Aunt Grace's personal papers. Our job was to hold the torch and to give Rebecca moral support. She could never do something this bad on her own.

Rebecca started by going through Aunt Grace's committee papers stacked on the shelf in the pantry. I told her she was nuts but she had read some Nancy Drews and knew to look in the obvious places. She patiently went through every scribbler. I pinched a couple of oatmeal cookies since we were in the pantry anyway, and then Kate and I flipped through the summer catalogues and had a good laugh over the foundation garments.

Rebecca was rattling the sugar and flour canisters when a letter fell on the counter. It had been pushed into a crevice under the shelf. She picked it up and we could all see the formal bank letterhead. Rebecca held on to it and then, with a fierceness I had never seen in her before, she told us to hush as she smoothed out the paper.

It was from Mr. Harris. In a nutshell, it said that if Rebecca were allowed to come to Boston, he would donate two thousand dollars to the St. James's Church Society. That was more money than we would earn in five years of times, raffles and turkey dinners. He also said that Rebecca had a rare talent and that it was Aunt Grace's duty to help her daughter develop it.

The handwriting was sparse and full of spaces, the paper thick and the ink black. Rebecca carefully put the letter back where she found it and with her chin set in a most unflattering jut, she headed up the stairs. I followed right behind and as we reached the upstairs landing it dawned on me that we might have cut off more than we could chew. Why was this Mr. Harris being so persistent?

We moved toward the back room at the head of the stairs, just to the left of the landing. It was opposite Aunt Grace and Uncle Wilf's bedroom. That door was very definitely shut.

The back room was always called the back room, but if we wanted to be fancy we could have called it the lavender room, after the color of the wood trim and the flowers in the wallpaper. Or it could have been called the scenic room because when you stood at the window and pulled back the lace curtains, you could see right down the harbor to Cook's Point. It could have been the linen room or the airing room, too. It was here that Aunt Grace stored her flannel sheets and her damask tablecloth, and it had a clothesline strung near the ceiling worked by a pulley. She dried her winter wash in the back room and aired blankets and woolens with the window open in the fall and the spring. There was a Singer sewing machine in front of the window and Aunt Grace's odds-and-ends box was on a small table beside it. So it could have been the sewing room, too. But it was the back room.

I had been in the back room lots of times, mostly when I was small, and I could remember every detail, especially the smell of old clothes, papers and wallpaper paste. Rebecca and I had been allowed to play house there as long as we didn't mess anything up.

Cardboard boxes were piled along one wall; stacked neatly, filled with old clothes and papers. They were all sizes—York canned peas, Cow Brand baking soda, Good Luck margarine, Purity Lemon Creams, Sifto salt, Cosby molasses, Cream of the West all-purpose flour and Sun Maid raisins. Rebecca knew what was in most of the boxes. She helped pack them and moved them for spring and fall cleanings. But she wanted to go through them again in case she had missed something. At first I thought this was too much work but my cousin only opened the tops and instantly recalled what exactly was in each carton. There were a couple of small ones near the bottom that she had never seen. We helped her get to them and saw the disappointment on her face when she found a stack of scribblers filled with accounts from the store and post office that Aunt Grace and Uncle Wilf ran years ago when Uncle Wilf was recovering from his war wounds.

It was dark. Uncle Wilf would be finished at the Lodge within the hour. He was a gentle dad but he wouldn't put up with us rummaging through stuff that was meant to be none of our business. Even I hated to get him angry. I was getting cold feet.

"Rebecca," I said. "I think that's it for tonight. Maybe we shouldn't poke around anymore. We'll come up with another plan." But she wasn't listening to me.

"I want you to stand here at the door while I go into Mom and Dad's room," she said. "My birth certificate has got to be in there. It's the only room I never go into in this house. Kate, you go downstairs and give us a holler when Dad is coming through the gate. Melinda, lend me the torch and stay by the door."

I opened my mouth to tell her she was going too far, but even in the darkness I could see a hard glint in her eyes and the firm set of her jaw. She was going in and there was no talking her out of it.

She twisted the cut glass doorknob and was in the room as quick as I could flutter my eyelashes. I saw the torchlight cross over a narrow iron bed covered in a white chenille bedspread. The single pillow was hidden by a lace shammy.

It confused me at first. My mind couldn't adjust to the knowledge that Aunt Grace, who was at least five foot ten, with a matronly figure, and Uncle Wilf who was well over six feet and as broad as a bull, could fit together in this Goldilocks bed.

Rebecca opened a wooden wardrobe. The hinges creaked and I almost jumped out of my skin. I saw shadows of a couple of dresses, Aunt Grace's winter coat and Uncle Wilf's Sunday suit and white shirt. Neat and tidy, no secret cubbies. Rebecca wasted no time there.

I followed my cousin's eyes across the room to another bed. It was against the far wall, a narrow homemade wooden daybed, neatly done up with a black-and-red check wool blanket and a rather flat pillow covered in a plain white linen case. The edges of the blanket were folded around the bed military-style. The bed was longer than most. There was no doubt who slept there.

The whole room was as neat as a pin, shipshape. Aunt Grace's good hat was on top of the wardrobe. Her dressing gown was on a hook on the wall beside the bed. The chamber pot under the washstand looked like it had never been used. The white-and-rose bowl and pitcher gleamed in the darkness and the white linen towels were starched and ironed. We could see the polished wood floor under both beds and there was absolutely nothing there. If I ever imagined a room in a nunnery, this would have been it.

I knew then why Rebecca didn't have a brother or sister. Oh, the question was on the tip of my tongue a few times but there never was a right time to ask.

I felt sick to my stomach. It was like the time retarded Jimmy kicked me or when my Matt first kissed me on the lips. But it was different too because I knew that by coming up the stairs and opening that door with Rebecca, I was peering into a very private life. I had learned something I didn't want to know and didn't need to know.

I whispered to Rebecca that Uncle Wilf would be home soon. She turned on her heel to follow my voice and as she did, she stumbled on a floorboard near the Goldilocks bed. Next thing I knew she was on the floor and pushing her nails down between the wide boards. Up came a pine plank and I heard her gasp.

I couldn't bear the suspense a moment longer and I rushed into the room to see what was going on. There, in a space under the floor, was a dust-covered cardboard box about the size of a family Bible.

I was close enough to Rebecca to see the moonlit beads of sweat on her upper lip.

"Uncle Wilf is almost here," shouted Kate from downstairs, and Rebecca and I grabbed each other in our utter fright. Sweet Jesus!

She pushed me away, snatched up the cardboard box, kicked the plank back in place, grasped my hand, pulled me out of the room and closed the door behind us. I was frozen to the landing but Rebecca ran to her room and came back empty-handed. We smoothed our blouses and our hair, ran down the stairs and by the time Uncle Wilf was in the kitchen, the kettle was on the stove, Rebecca was measuring out sugar, the lamp flooded the room and we were into some silly chat about something or other. For the life of me I can't remember a word of what we said.

◦

Most folks in the Cove would have said we were a bunch of heathens for being so wild. The way I look at it is that someone Up There must have wanted us to find that box. How else would Rebecca have stubbed her toe in the dark on just the right spot?

Uncle Wilf went off to bed because he was going fishing in about five hours' time and after that he had to go to get Aunt Grace in Beach Cove. He told us to be good little girls. He was mischievous like that, my Uncle Wilf. He was the only adult in the harbor who still went mummering at Christmas. Everyone knew who he was under the white sheets and old hats because he could never hide his vast height. But they played along because he was silly enough to dress up like a woman and give them all a bit of fun. It was breaking my heart to deceive him.

By this time it was eleven-thirty and we still had some dirty business to do. Rebecca was putting a pan of sugar, evaporated milk and cocoa on the stove.

"What are you doing, maid?" I asked her. It sure was a strange time to be making fudge.

"This is Dad's favorite. Since I'm up I might as well be doing something useful." It was her way of making amends for the harm we were about to do.

When we heard Uncle Wilf's door close, we told Kate about the cardboard box and she, being a city girl without morals, volunteered to go through it as soon as Uncle Wilf was asleep. Rebecca was stalling and I was none too sure myself anymore. I'd done some bad things in my day but I never hurt nobody or put my nose into something as awesome as this. Then I remembered another Cove maxim—"An open door would tempt a saint."

The fudge was soon bubbling on the stove and Rebecca beat it to a gloss and poured it on a buttered plate. We had to fish or cut bait.

Rebecca went upstairs. She was gone for a couple of minutes and Kate and I hardly breathed.

She came back with the box held tight against her chest. Taking a closer look I saw it was the kind of box fancy writing paper used to come in. It was about a foot square and half a foot deep. Someone had taken the trouble to cover it with faded cabbage roses, a wallpaper from years ago.

Rebecca laid it on the scrubbed kitchen table.

"We just can't open it here in the middle of the kitchen, maid," I said. "What if someone looks in the lace curtains?" This was unlikely but you could see how strange we were getting. We looked around for a safe spot. Kate broke the tension with a giggle and the suggestion we go down the hall to the outhouse.

It was an inspired idea. My aunt and uncle had the snazziest toilet in the Cove. The house backed onto the beach and the ingenious thing about the design of their saltbox was the bump-out two-seater—boys and girls—that sat out over the water at high tide. Aunt Grace wallpapered it every spring and this year there were pink and white carnations climbing the walls. When the tide was out, it was a bit of a mess down there (if you wanted to look) but when the tide came in, the toilet got one big flush—at least twice a day. They never had to get up in the dark of night and race across the yard like the rest of us. Lots of folks were green with envy over that toilet.

The tide was up, the smell was fresh-washed and there was no chance that any wayward kids would be sneaking around on the beach. The thud of the waves hitting the breakwater would drown out our voices. Being out back meant I could smoke and I did like to smoke when I was as nervous as a lobster in boiling water.

The three of us squeezed in. When we put both covers down, there was enough room for me and Kate to sit with our backs against the east and west walls and for Rebecca to sit on the floor facing us with the box in between the two seats.

"Lord dyin', open the darn box," I said. "I can't stand it another second." I aimed the torch onto the dusty lid.

Rebecca took off the cover and we could see right away that we had hit the jackpot. There were official-looking stamps and signatures and the manila envelopes used by the government and the school. Each envelope was neatly slit with a knife, each fold was perfect, done once, good and sharp.

The thick white paper on top was Rebecca's confirmation certificate. Digging down but being careful to keep everything in order, we found Uncle Wilf's discharge papers from the British navy, his navy medical papers, the stub of a train ticket from Boston, and Aunt Grace and Uncle Wilf's marriage certificate stamped in Halifax. Aunt Grace's signature was cool and elegant, just what you'd expect. Uncle Wilf had marked a simple X. His hand must have been wounded.

While I was looking at the marriage certificate, Rebecca pulled out her report card from first grade.

"Look," she said. "I got all As. Can you imagine Mom keeping this?"

Kate marked the spot and pulled out an envelope with old family photos. A picture of Nan and Granddad in their wedding clothes, the same one that was on the table in Aunt Grace's parlor. Then another picture of Nan and Granddad, older and with three children tucked around them, eyes wide and staring. The photo was scorched around the edges like it had been in a fire. There was Aunt Grace, about fourteen years old, her nose too big for her face, just the way mine was a year ago. My mom was a pretty enough youngster standing, looking up at her mother and in between them, on Nan's lap, Herb's baby mouth was shut tight but he looked like a little rascal anyway.

"Wait a minute," said Kate. "That baby looks like my dad but it can't be him. He's a year younger than Aunt Grace. This boy is about two years old. He still has his ringlets for goodness' sake. I've never seen this photo before, have you?"

She was right. I had never laid eyes on it. Herb came in between the two sisters. No way on earth could this be Herb.

I thought of that old proverb we learned in Sunday school. *Oh what a tangled web we weave when first we practice to deceive.*

While Kate and I were stuck on the photo, Rebecca was holding something that was making her keep her mouth open rather unattractively.

"What have you got there, Rebecca?" I said as I reached over to take it out of her hands. She simply dropped the piece of paper and it floated into my lap. I took a quick look. "Sweet Jesus," I whispered. Even Kate, who had her eyes peeled on the family photo, realized something bigger was happening.

"Did you see the dates?" Rebecca asked. "My birthday is September tenth. Melinda, you are the eldest by three weeks, and then it's Kate's birthday in March. That's what we've always been told. This says I was born September tenth, all right, but look, a year earlier."

We looked at each other in pure amazement.

Rebecca made a miserable joke. "I see now why Mom doesn't want me to go to Boston. My birth certificate alone would set some tongues on hinges. Can you see me handing around my new passport in the Cove?"

I unfurled myself from the toilet seat and put my arms around her shoulders. She crumpled against me.

"This can't be right, it must be a mistake," I said softly.

I wanted to hold her forever but it was time we got a move on.

"We've got to get the box back in the cubbyhole before your mom comes home. We'll put everything in the way we found it. You have to put it back when your dad goes fishing," I said. Rebecca was like a rag doll so Kate and I carefully stacked all the papers in the box.

"I'll stay with you tonight," Kate said to Rebecca, as her body began shaking with big wet sobs.

That suited me very well indeed, because I'd managed to sneak Rebecca's birth certificate under my sweater and I'd seen enough to know that there was more out of whack than Rebecca's year of birth.

CHAPTER FIVE

❧

The older the crab, the tougher the claws

I raced up the road and into our lane like the devil was on my tail. The paper was hot coals close to my skin. Everyone was in bed and I was able to get to my room without being asked if I was sick with a fever.

I studied the certificate by the moonlight and couldn't make hide nor hair out of it. None of the dates matched up with what I saw on the marriage certificate, and Rebecca's birth certificate was issued in Boston, not Halifax.

It was too much to take in so I pushed it back into its envelope and put it in my bottom drawer under my winter step-ins. I tossed and turned all night.

The next afternoon, Nan was in the kitchen making a batch of jam from a load of raspberries Georgie and Flossie picked up on the hillside behind the house. While she put beans to soak for the next day, me and Kate and Georgie and Flossie cleaned the berries and pretty soon Nan was measuring out white sugar and heaping the ripe red fruit in a cast iron pot on the hot stove. Nan sent Kate to the back shed to clean a few Mason jars and lids and she asked the twins to run to the store for more sugar.

This was the best time of day. The men were safe in the harbor. Most of the backbreaking work was done and they were chewing tobacco and smoking pipes and hand-rolled cigarettes as they mended nets and rested before tending to tomorrow's supply of bait. The women were at home, getting the supper ready. The vegetable gardens were weeded, the washing and ironing done, the bread baked, the floors scrubbed, the fresh fish claimed from the men for the family meal, visits done, sick children tucked in on the kitchen daybeds.

I floured the fish while Nan fried up bits of salt pork and kept an eye on the jam cooking on the back burner.

"Nan," I said as the day cooled off and the bluebottle flies dove against the back screen door, driven mad by the smell of dead fish. "Did you ever want to leave Cook's Cove?"

"Why would I ever want to leave here?" she asked. "Sure there were tough times but we managed. We were lucky that the fishing has mostly been good in these waters, there's a little bit of fertile land and the meadows can feed as many sheep and cows as we've needed. And there are lots of berries. The house is still solid. Can't think what else I would have wanted."

I gave her a good look-over. Like I was seeing her for the first time. Her curved back was turned to me as she fiddled with the supper. There she was, a once-tall woman with white hair pulled back in a severe bun wearing a gray shirtwaist dress, a clean white apron made out of flour sacks and embroidered with tiny pink roses, and black socks running over the tops of her black lace-up pumps. She lifted a pot of boiling potatoes and I saw the skinny elbows and the narrow veins in her neck.

I saw the woman who cooked our meals, washed our clothes and reminded us to sit up straight. In the evening, when Mom was home, she stole into the shadows, absorbed in her hooked rugs, her darning and her knitting. In Cook's Cove she was a wise elder, a woman listened to because she worked hard, had once had her own business, raised a family as a young widow, and was a Derby.

But she hadn't always been this old woman. Her beginnings were humble but for a few years she wore silk and lace, ordered her china from Boston and her hand soap from New York.

She was the only child of an elderly father and sickly mother. She was always clever with her hands and knit all the warm clothes for her family by the time she was ten. A year later she was making rugs to sell, doing all the housework and drying her father's fish. They lived across the harbor near Cook's Point, always apart from the Cove people. It was rough getting to school in the winter—the harbor ice wasn't always stable—so she learned to read and write using the Bible and the Farmers' Almanac. Life was hard but she knew no different and, as I've often heard her say, the Lord gave her the strength to carry on. The family had a couple of good years of fishing and a couple of bad ones. More fish meant more work in the summer; fewer fish meant more work in the winter making ends meet.

When she was fourteen there was a terrible winter after a bad fishing season. Storm after storm, high winds, layers of ice on the roof, so cold the water barrel froze in the kitchen. In February the salt cod and all the berries she had spent weeks picking and bottling in the fall were gone. Her dad went out every day to snare rabbits and shoot whatever seabirds he could find.

Then, on a morning that was steeped in an ice fog, he

didn't come back. Three days later, her mom, who had seldom been out of her bed for two years, died, probably from the cold, the hunger and whatever illness was eating her body. Nan, who was Mildred Snooks back then, waited another day and night for her dad and then she tramped six miles through deep snow around the harbor to the big house where old Captain Derby lived. Her dad had talked about the Captain's fairness when he'd gone sealing for him up on the Labrador. She told us about coming into this house with the fire roaring, ginger cookies coming out of the oven, and the kitchen cheerfully dressed in blue check curtains with a matching tablecloth. She could barely open her mouth. Mrs. Derby got her a cup of tea and a plate of toast. Then Mildred was ashamed because in drinking the tea and gobbling down the toast, she had forgotten her poor mom and dad. She burst into tears and blurted out the story.

The Derbys were very kind. They put her to bed in a warm room with stacks of feather quilts and rounded up neighbors to tend to her mother and to form a search party to find her dad. They looked for days before they gave up. Her dad's body was washed ashore the next spring. The only thing left from her mother was a cut glass sugar bowl that we still had on our sideboard. She stayed with the Derbys the rest of the winter and paid her keep by helping the Captain's wife with the chores.

The Derbys had one child who survived childhood, a grown son who worked as a captain on sealing boats off the Labrador coast in the spring, sailed cargo boats in the Caribbean in the fall and winter and in the summer came home to help his dad with his shipping business. The Derbys moved all the fish and supplies between the Bay of Islands and St. John's.

Captain Joe took an instant liking to the skinny redhead

who had come to live in the big house while he was away. She did the cleaning, cooked the meals and was obviously devoted to his mother. He had an eye for a pretty girl all right but there was always so much work and responsibility that there had been no time for serious courting.

He was called Young Captain Derby but Mildred could see he wasn't really young anymore. Joe was thirty-two. She was fifteen. He worked from dawn on the water and started coming home for supper promptly at four. He eased Mildred from serving the meals to joining them at the table. He helped her plant a herb garden of tansy, mint and chives and he brought her lilac bushes from the Mainland. He gathered rhubarb and cleaned it while she made pastry. He brought her wild columbine, lilies, daisies and the roses from out back. He helped her weed the potato patch, a job no decent man would be caught doing in broad daylight. At the garden party he bid a ridiculous amount for her boxed picnic when it was auctioned and the whole Cove knew the lay of his heart. He asked her to marry him that night after the dance by saying, "Us two will do, won't we?" She said yes.

The old Captain and Mrs. Derby happily made room for Mildred, the new daughter they already loved. Joe was away a lot with the boats but Mildred was blessed with easy pregnancies, easy deliveries and happy robust children. Life was good in the big house. There was food enough for the family and for anyone else who needed it. There was money for clothes and china ordered from St. John's and the States, even a beaver coat. Nan had a mahogany sideboard shipped from London and each of the children had a Sunday outfit of good silk. She had a husband she loved and who loved her. You could tell that from the way she talked about him.

The old Captain and his wife died at home in the front bedroom upstairs within a week of one another. A year later

Captain Joe went out the harbor on a rescue mission during a November gale and never came back.

The whole Cove turned out to tell Mildred how brave Joe had been. She thought he had been plain foolish. He had youngsters and as far as she was concerned should never have gone off to find a drunken fisherman in a storm. The Captain's death was a shock all right but an even bigger shock was finding out that she was responsible for six new boats he had ordered from Nova Scotia and as she started to pull things together, most of the world headed into the big depression.

The boats were sold at a heavy loss but she kept the house and the family together by calling on her earlier life and her old fish and rug-making skills. She sent Herb off to the city to work in the paper mill and taught the girls how to survive on nothing. She sold her knitting and rugs to a fancy shop in St. John's.

The war saved them. Suddenly the world needed fish and with Mae and Grace working alongside her on the flakes and in the fish plant, and Herb sending home money, she could finally get the roof and chimney fixed and buy glass for the broken windows. Soon they were comfortable again.

This was the woman who was the first one out of bed every morning, who blew out the lamp at night. The woman who most often slept on the daybed in the kitchen because, she said, she didn't sleep well and didn't want to wake the family. Who, we knew in truth, wanted to be in the kitchen to get a warm fire going at daylight. She had never left the harbor.

Nan's one failing was that she sometimes turned inside herself and didn't let anyone in. Whenever a storm hovered, she sat in her rocker in the window for hours and hours, staring out to sea. We made sure she had lots of tea heaped with sugar when she went silent and moody on us.

After going through the secret box, I knew something else about my nan. I knew there was a baby, younger than my mother, who looked like my Uncle Herb and who had disappeared from the much-talked about family history. Strange things, families. They smack you in the face just when you aren't expecting it.

But I had to leave all that alone because I was on a fishing expedition of another kind. Once I had cozied up to Nan and got on her good side, I came right out and asked her about when Rebecca and my Aunt Grace came back to Cook's Cove. She wasn't the least bit suspicious.

"Sure, you know the story, Melinda," she said. "You were about four at the time and I bet you can even remember some of it. We were so excited about having Grace and Wilf come home with their little girl. We hadn't seen Grace for such a long time and she looked so lovely getting off the boat in a red wool coat with a fur collar and matching hat. No one else played the church organ like she did and Wilf's house was half-finished and looked so sorrowful. And I wanted to see my granddaughter Rebecca. They've become the big family here, like we used to be. Between you and me, my only sadness is that they only ever had the one child. Herb had a gang of children and your mom had her reasons for having only the three, but I always thought Grace and Wilf should have had a houseful, not just the one."

If you fished long enough, you were bound to get a nibble. My nan knew nothing about the sleeping arrangements Down Below and what was this about my mother? I'd never thought about it before, why we were only three when my mom and dad were married for eleven years when he died. That was time enough for half a dozen at least. My dad loved children. He was always holding me on his lap, and taking me down to the fish stage, and making up songs about little girls who liked to talk too much.

But my nan wasn't going to let the cat out of the bag on Aunt Grace. Her memory was like the fog on the Grand Banks. I badgered her some more, asking about Rebecca's upcoming birthday, about Rebecca being born in Halifax, about when, exactly, Aunt Grace and Uncle Wilfred were married. She was vague about dates. It was clear they meant nothing to her. Finally Nan shooed me out of the kitchen by telling me to go find Kate who she said must have fallen down the toilet.

❧

I was in a bit of a bitchy mood the next day because my feet got sore from wearing my spike heels around the Cove all morning as I sold raffle tickets on a ribbon-and-velvet fancy cushion done up by Nan and six-quart bottles of moose meat donated by the Orange Lodge. If you make the rounds expecting people to give yet again to the church, you've got to give them a bit of dazzle. So I suffered with the heels and wore a freshly starched cotton sundress with a stiff crinoline and a silver locket borrowed from Mom, which I put back in her secret hideaway as soon as I got home so there wouldn't be any misunderstandings. I was missing my Matt too. He was pretty scarce because he and his dad had gone to their summer camp. And it was hard to be jolly me when the chance of a visit to Boston was fading as fast as the light on a December's day. It's true I'd never wanted to go to Boston before but once it had been offered I was feeling like Cinderella after the ball.

I was down to visit Rebecca a few times and she was just moping around, hardly paying attention to her chores. She was trying to get up enough nerve to have it out with her mother about her birth date. I was worried the whole thing was going too far.

I was right in the mood to go after my mom as soon as she walked in the door from her shift at the fish plant.

I was just about to lay into her when the back door opened again and Aunt Grace walked in.

Lordy, lordy, you could have knocked me over with a gull feather. What with my mom working at the fish plant all hours of the day and night and Aunt Grace running the Cove, there were no morning mug-ups for the two sisters. Aunt Grace only came by when she was collecting for something or needed Mom's help in the church and sometimes on Sunday afternoon to see Nan. My mom went Down Below when someone in the Cove asked her to ask Grace for something. My aunt put most people in a tremble and it was often up to my mom to find the right words to get the right answer. We went to Grace's twice a year as a family. She made Christmas dinner for the whole crowd and she invited the lot of us to her house for a social evening of hymn singing when it was Nan's birthday in April. This arrangement made us the only family in the Cove who had to wait for an invite. I couldn't remember the last time she dropped in for no reason.

A handkerchief was balled in her hand and her hatpin was sticking straight up, a sure sign she came away in a hurry.

"Mae," she said, "I need to talk to you. Can we go into the parlor?"

La-di-da! The parlor, no less. This was big time. The room was only ever used for funerals and weddings.

My mom doused her Export A, dropped the dish towel she was just about to tie around her waist and almost choked on the sip of tea she slurped as she rushed to the front room on the heels of her big sister. The parlor door shut and Kate was at my side.

"I've never seen Aunt Grace so agitated. Do you think she knows something?"

Almost at the same moment the back door rattled again and it was Rebecca. It was beginning to feel like a church picnic in our house.

"Is my mom here?" she whispered. We signaled that her mom and my mom were across the hall. She rolled her eyes upwards and we sneaked up the back stairs. We got to my room desperate with curiosity.

"Me and Mom just had a deuce of a fight about Boston. I was screaming at her that I had to go and she wouldn't even talk to me. The more I screamed, the quieter she got. It was awful."

"Back up, start at the beginning," ordered Kate.

A telegram had come for Aunt Grace and Rebecca was just able to see that it came from Boston before her mom tossed it in the stove unopened and carried on like nothing had happened. That got Rebecca real mad. The dam broke when her mom came in and said she was organizing a celebration for the road coming through for September. The minister of transportation could only come on one day, the tenth. So her mom said it would have to be the tenth and that she was sorry that Rebecca's sixteenth birthday was turning out to be such a busy day. Aunt Grace was going upstairs when Rebecca said something like, "It don't matter, I could easily skip another birthday." Her mom stopped cold and said, "What an odd thing to say, my dear. I'm sure we can arrange something for the eleventh." Rebecca could see she was a little rattled and jumped in and told Grace that if she would only change her mind about art school, there was still time to plan it all out. But Grace came to her wits real quick. She turned on Rebecca and said, real angry and real low, "We will not talk about this ever again. You are not going to Boston."

That was when our Rebecca got nasty herself.

"I figured I had nothing to lose," she said. "I screamed that me and Melinda and Kate knew a few things about her that maybe she didn't want anyone else to know. Maybe, I said, she might want to think about Boston again."

By this time Rebecca was wiping up her tears with my second prettiest lace hankie. I wanted to tell her thanks for dragging us into this but it was not the time.

"She sent me to my room and the next thing I'm screaming that I was only good for all the work I did around here. I said all kinds of stuff that I can't even remember anymore. The next thing I knew she was putting on her coat and hat and going out."

There was a way of hearing every word spoken in the parlor. I knew about it because Georgie and Flossie were able to repeat my Matt's first proposal of marriage to everyone around the supper table. The parlor backed onto the old bookkeeping office that hadn't been used since the boat business was sold off. It was once heated by connecting a pipe through the wall to an ancient oil stove in the parlor. The stove died and the pipe fell out years ago. Nan simply papered over the hole.

We crept down the back staircase, crossed the narrow hall and slipped into the back room. We could hear the same as if we were sitting on the dusty green velvet humpback couch right beside my mother and my aunt.

Aunt Grace was talking.

"Those girls are up to something and I've had enough of their nonsense. I think your Melinda is making trouble again. All this gossip going around about Rebecca being offered a chance to go to Boston. That was between me and Mr. Harris. Then Rebecca had the nerve to question my decision. And Rebecca is wasting her summer instead of reading her textbooks for grade eleven. This afternoon she was so rude to me I didn't recognize the daughter I've worked very hard to bring up as a young Christian lady."

Mom answered with her soft and gentle approach. "It's terrible the way things are changing and—" Aunt Grace cut her off.

"Things are not changing. Melinda is a bad influence. You're never here to properly keep an eye on her and Nan is too soft. Here's what I think we should do. We have a little over a week. The reverend told me just yesterday that the Young Christian Ladies' Summer Prayer Camp at Copper Cove is not full. I'm pretty sure I can get Rebecca and Melinda in starting next Saturday for a month. Kate can go home on Friday's boat. Her mom won't want her going to a Protestant camp."

"I just don't know," said my mom. "I can't tell Melinda what to do. She is a grown woman with a mind of her own."

"That's the problem, Mae," said Aunt Grace. "You're letting her take charge of her life and your life. They're children and they should be treated like children. I want the girls away to camp on Friday. There is no time to waste."

She walked toward the door. Her forceful footsteps were softened by the old rug but we could still tell she was angry. This was the way it had been for as long as I could remember. Grace knew what was right and good and she told my mother and my mother did whatever she was told, mostly.

Aunt Grace always had it in for me. Only last fall she blamed me when she found a stack of drawings in Rebecca's room of my Matt without his shirt on. He was all rippling muscle. Now for sure I knew about the drawings because she did them while my Matt was chopping our wood and we were sitting on the woodpile to keep him company. Aunt Grace gave my mom a tongue-lashing about how wicked I was and ordered that like Rebecca, I had to stay in my room for a week. The old biddy. Mom didn't stand up to her. She had seen the drawings too and had told Rebecca they were wonderful. I was sent to my room right there and then—four o'clock in the afternoon. Later Mom came up with a plate of Purity jam-jams. She mentioned that since she was working the evening shift at the plant, she wouldn't be checking on my whereabouts. That's the way she dealt with her sister when they disagreed. She didn't argue, she endured. She said life was more peaceful that way.

The door opened and already Kate and Rebecca had turned away from the wall. It was then I heard Grace say, "You owe me, Mae. Just remember that." A second later my aunt was gone.

We were as quiet as snails going back upstairs. We flopped onto the beds and were numb. The older the crab, the tougher the claws.

We knew that my mom was not going to stand up to Grace. And once we were at camp my mom wouldn't be able to do a thing. Our fate was sealed.

And, I thought, what exactly was Grace talking about, my mom owed her? Owed her what?

CHAPTER SIX

❧

Three people can keep a secret, if two of them are dead

My aunt seemed to think that I came up with the master plans for mischief and that my two cousins just went along for the fun. She was right, of course, but we never let on. My cousins shared the blame, so my aunt was never absolutely certain. She never liked my wicked smile and always believed I would come to no good.

Take for example the summer when we were thirteen and I suggested we row to Black's Harbour for the garden party and time there. *Row*, for crying out loud. It was fifteen miles there and fifteen miles back. We didn't tell our moms because we thought we'd be home in time to sneak into bed and they'd be none the wiser. We got there but we didn't do any dancing. The blood dripping from our blistered hands was none too pretty. Rebecca found us a place to stay for the night and then sent a telegram to Cook's Cove. Aunt Grace arranged for the ferry to stop in at Black's Harbour and give us a tow home. The most embarrassing hours of my life. Aunt Grace found time to tell me not to do anything that stupid again.

Then last summer's hijinks got tongues wagging. And, Lord dyin', we were innocent. Aunt Grace asked the three of us to give the church a special scrub. You couldn't say no to the lady, so we got brooms and mops and buckets and headed up to the crest of the hill after dinner. I had slipped a tiny silver-tone AM/FM transistor radio in my apron pocket. After a couple of hours, my Matt and Chas found us sweating a river. I flopped down into the last pew, ate the Caramel Log bars my Matt brought along, turned up the radio and in two clicks we were all dancing up a storm to "Jailhouse Rock." We were never too tired to dance. Then the music changed.

"Hey, Kate," I shouted. "What are you doing to your poor body?" She was sliding under a broomstick stretched between two pews.

"It's the limbo," she said. "Everyone's doing it, you retard."

A moment later the big oak door crashed shut and we could hear someone outside slamming into the brackets the slab of wood that kept the door protected from Atlantic gale force winds. We shouted and screamed but the upshot was that we were stuck in the church until Aunt Grace couldn't find Rebecca and she came looking for her. She spied my radio and none of us could hold our heads up for days because of the stories of what we must have been up to in the House of God. Aunt Grace forbade Rebecca to see me for two weeks.

Toward the end of the summer we found out that Jimmy, the boy up our lane who was not right in the head, was spying on us and had a fit when he heard Kate say "retard." He thought she was calling him that, so he slammed the door shut and ran around telling people we were doing nasty things in the church. It took a long time to live that one down.

So it was no wonder that Aunt Grace was blaming me again. Rebecca was a bit dazed about being sent off to church camp, but she knew enough to get home before her mom. She was out the back door and over the fence as fast as a wild stallion.

No sooner were mother and daughter gone than my mom came to my bedroom and turned on me, real vicious.

"Now, young ladies, I don't want no lies. You have been up to no good and you had better tell me what's going on. You'll stay in this room until I hear every word." Her voice was low and dangerous. She was a sweetie, but she had her boiling point.

Kate tried to sneak out and go downstairs, for a glass of water, she said. Like a rat deserting a sinking ship. Mom caught her by the arm a bit hard. Kate was surprised enough to stop in her tracks.

"No, Kate, you stay too. I expect you're in on this some-how. I saw the looks going around the kitchen when Grace came in. If I don't get to the bottom of this you'll be going home on Friday's boat."

Oh, my mom was being very nasty. We were cornered.

I cleared my throat, fluffed up the fancy cushions on my bed, straightened my rose chenille bedspread, tidied a bunch of *Teen Confessions* and kept going over in my head just how much to tell my mother. I started by warning her that she might not want to hear the whole story.

"None of that, you hear. I want the truth." By this time her eyes were blazing.

I thought of the old saying that my nan drummed into me as a little girl. Three people can keep a secret—if two of them are dead. With my mom standing in front of us, hands on her thin hips, tapping her toes, jaw tense, I realized that three people could never keep a secret. I decided it was best to come clean and get Mom to help us out of this mess.

It took a few minutes to tell about us going to search for the birth certificate. Mom started to dust my bureau with the corner of her apron and she moved my picture of Jimmy Dean so I knew she was agitated.

I went on to explain that Rebecca was pretty upset about her mom changing her birth date like that and never telling her. I also told her that sooner or later one of us had to tell Aunt Grace before it was whispered everywhere. It was bound to happen. If everything was out in the open, I suggested, perhaps me and Rebecca could still get to Boston in time for the art course. In fact, I said, perhaps it was better if we were away to give it all a chance to blow over.

My mom quickly moved on to straighten my glossy photograph of Ricky Nelson and then turned and lashed into me with a vehemence I had never seen.

"Whatever you think you know, none of us knows anything. Understand? It's bad enough that you girls went snooping. None of this leaves this room. You, too, Kate. One word of this to anyone and you'll see just how miserable I can make your lives. The Derbys do not wash their dirty linen in public. This is what families are for. We stick together." With that outburst she turned on her heel and left our room.

Me and Kate meekly went downstairs to help get supper on the table and we could hardly look at each other because of our burning shame. My mom had got us right between the eyes.

After midnight I was still awake. I heard Mom tossing and turning in her bedroom down the hall and I figured it was time to skin the old cow. I was never shy about meeting disaster head on.

"What is it now, Melinda? I'm awake more than I'm asleep these days. Come in, get in bed, the nights are getting some chilly already."

"What I really want to know is what Aunt Grace said today."

"I thought you'd be asking," she said. "I've not been able to sleep because I knew I would have to talk to you and I don't know what to say. You're a smart young woman, but my sister thinks you and Kate and Rebecca are children. It's hard to know what to do. Maybe you are children and you've tricked me. I shouldn't even be talking to you like this. I should just make up my mind. But I'm not that kind of mother, never was. I can't even stay mad at you for a whole day."

I gave her a big squeeze and she gave me the goods on the session in the parlor. I acted surprised and then got brazen.

"No way am I going to any church camp for young ladies," I said. "You and Nan taught me all I need to know about being a Christian. It wouldn't work anyway. I'd do a little cussing and I'd be out of there in a flash. And I don't imagine they'd like me sneaking off with my Matt after dark. Aunt Grace didn't reckon that the church camp is only a mile or two along the shore from my Matt's fishing camp. Tell Aunt Grace I'm not going." She held my clenched shoulders and got me to calm down. I was close to tears and being so close to my mom and all I felt my eyelids getting itchy.

"Mom," I said, sniffling, "there's something else you should know."

"What else could there possibly be?" she asked.

I thought I could hold my secret in but it was pushing through my skin. Secrets do that.

"We know that Rebecca's birth date is different. Rebecca saw it, I saw it and so did Kate. But I saw a couple of other things. Did you know that Rebecca was born in Boston, not Halifax? And did you know that Uncle Wilf is not put down as her father? The man's name was Henry Ellis. Have you ever heard of him?"

I could tell when my mom was shocked. She scrunched her nose and her eyebrows disappeared under her bangs. But she let me go on.

I said it wasn't fair that something that happened sixteen years ago was standing in the way of a different life for Rebecca and perhaps even me. I loved my Matt and I knew I would marry him, but I wanted to heal people too and I was starting to think I could do both. Aunt Grace kept up her nursing after she was married, for goodness' sake. I didn't know how to say what was in my heart but Mom understood anyway.

She told me that all she ever wanted for me was the chance to use my brains. The Derby women had always been smart, she claimed. She got excited about how the government was hiring nurses for new clinics being built out along the new road around the Bay of Islands and about the Victorian Order of Nurses who worked a lot with new mothers and their babies. We talked about the article on the VON in last fall's *Chatelaine*. I guessed for the first time that it was no mistake that the magazine was left open on the kitchen table.

"The new road will mean you can live in the Cove and be responsible for two or three communities. And, honey, of course you can be a nurse and be married. I read somewhere that lots of rural nurses have families nowadays. We're living in different times." She was beaming.

Maybe it was just a fuzzy dream but I was glad she felt that way and I told her so.

"Melinda, what have we got to do?" said my mom.

In one way or another she had been asking me that same question ever since Daddy died. She was as strong as a whale when it came to standing for those ten-hour freezing cold shifts down at the plant but she could never make a decision about anything important. Even at Daddy's wake, she sat up straight and solemn on a wooden chair in the parlor, seven months along with the twins, while me, Nan and Aunt Grace arranged the casket, the grave site, the flowers, the hymns and the sandwiches. She didn't even cry.

She had depended on me ever since to get the twins ready for their first day at school, to decide when any of us needed to go into Corner Brook to see a doctor, what to do about Nan when she had one of her fits, what bill to pay first and could we afford to have the roof fixed this summer or wait until next. Now this.

I told her that Rebecca was spun tight as an anchor in deep water. I told her we were wrong to go through Aunt Grace's things but that the cat was out of the bag now and that's all there was to it. I told her she had to get Aunt Grace to explain things to Rebecca, to clear the air and even to convince Aunt Grace that the paperwork for visiting the States could be done in the city and that there was no harm in Rebecca learning a little bit about drawing. Besides, with Rebecca being born in the States, maybe she didn't even need any papers to cross the border. I said she might as well find out about this Henry Ellis while she was at it. And, I said, she had to do it soon because the days were galloping along. I made her promise.

My mom nodded solemnly. Then she hustled me back to bed saying she had a lot of hard thinking to do.

We didn't know then what little time we had.

CHAPTER SEVEN

❧

Red sails in the morning
Sailors take warning

There was a big rush on lobster two days later, and my mom started working eighteen-hour shifts splitting, cooking and canning. That way she managed to avoid a heart-to-heart with Aunt Grace. But the delay created enough time for Rebecca to do one of the most foolish things she had ever done.

I awoke on Friday morning to a chill in my room. Kate was snuggled down under a quilt after getting in so late the night before that even the tomcats were finished their business. She had been seeing a lot of Chas since the dance, even slipping out back that time to clean Mason jars and meeting him for a wag over the back fence. For a plain girl with ugly glasses she was doing all right.

I had avoided Rebecca all week because I didn't know what to say to her. But I figured it was time to tell her that even if she got shipped off to camp, me and Kate were staying put in the Cove.

The harbor was calm and high clouds were swollen with

the pink light of the sunrise. Kate and I dressed in silence and came down the back stairs to the kitchen where Georgie and Flossie were playing. It looked like they were settling in for the day. The fire in the woodstove was a smoldering mass of spidery red embers. I tossed a junk of birch in and moved the kettle over the burner so we could have a mug of tea. My mom had gone to work. There was a note on the table telling me to make up a batch of pancakes.

Something was not quite right but it didn't click until I saw Nan rocking in the window. It meant there was a hard blow coming and Nan would be spending the day in her chair. We didn't get many summer storms so it was a surprise to see my nan quivering like a bowl of crabapple jelly. The weather looked fine to me, hardly anything except a gentle breeze from the east. I made the tea and brought Nan a mug and a biscuit. She ate and drank without a word. She didn't take her eyes off the harbor.

I thought about my Matt out fishing and turned an eye toward the heavens and asked the Almighty to take care of him. My nan was never wrong about a storm. With Mom off to work and Nan set for the day in her rocking chair, either myself or Kate had to stay put to keep an eye on the twins. The other would have the job of telling Rebecca we were not going to camp with her.

Over raisin pancakes and molasses we remembered this was the day each year that Aunt Grace set aside to clean the church. The lady liked giving it an absolutely thorough going-over all by herself once a year and the day was carved in stone—two weeks after the time and two weeks before Memorial Sunday, the day the whole Cove spent remembering our dead. Uncle Wilf was away too. As luck would have it he had been asked to help one of the young men choose the wood for a new boat. Uncle Wilf loved to build boats and was always helping someone to get a boat started by picking out the best trees with just the right curve to them. This time he was over in the next harbor.

Kate volunteered to keep an eye on the kiddies. The coward. I checked to see if we could manage without making a batch of bread and decided we could. Kate's bread was pitiful. City girls had no feel for it. I reminded her to keep giving Nan tea and some grub, took my Fair Isle sweater off the hook near the back door and I was away.

The morning light was uncanny. It was golden with splashes of pink and every blade of grass along the sides of the lane was glowing. It was mornings like this that I knew why my Matt and me were not rushing off to the city. I saw that the gulls were flying high. Not a good sign in weather lore.

It was still early so I was not surprised that the side door to my aunt and uncle's house was shut tight. I lifted the latch and let myself in. I flopped on the daybed and waited for Rebecca to come from the toilet or wherever she was hiding. I drummed my fingers against the iron frame and waited some more. Finally I went to the bottom of the stairs and shouted up. "Yoo-hoo, anybody home? It's your favorite cousin." No answer. She must be down at the fish. I carefully shut the door behind me and ran the two minutes to the Derby fishing stage.

There was no one around except old Johnny Pumphrey, who was half blind and as deaf as a doornail. I shouted at the top of my lungs asking him if he'd seen Rebecca.

He finally understood and I had to bend real low to hear him say that there'd be no fish drying today because of the storm. As blind and as deaf as he was, he knew a storm was coming, just like Nan did.

So where in the heck was Rebecca? I asked myself. I went back to her house and decided to take a closer look.

I went upstairs. I tapped lightly on my aunt and uncle's bedroom door. There were no sounds through the door and it would have taken more nerve than even I had to turn that knob. I went to Rebecca's bedroom just down the hall. She wasn't there, nor in the front guest bedroom where the reverend slept when he had to stay overnight in the Cove. I went to the back bedroom and was standing near the window when my eye caught movement. The harbor was spread out before me and the water was calm, reflecting the brooding mountains.

Lord jumpin' dyin'. Uncle Wilf's yellow rowboat was out on the water, and if I could trust my eyes, Rebecca was in it heading toward Cook's Point. I turned ever so slightly and just over the eastern hills I could see a black line, as thin as eyebrow pencil, moving toward the harbor from out along the Bay. On one side of the line, where Rebecca was rowing, the golden sun was shining, it was a beautiful day. Behind the line the clouds were black and thunderous and the rain was as thick as blowing sand.

Sacred Heart of Mary. It took me a split second to realize that Rebecca was rowing with her back to the squall line and couldn't see it. She was rowing right into the storm.

She was taking the long way around the point. Under normal conditions it was the right thing to do because it was easier for one person to land a boat on the pebble beach near our cave than risk hitting the rocks along the shore near the Neck. Even at high tide you needed two people there to give the rocks a miss. But to go around the point she had to go through the narrows, into the open water. The currents there were powerful and deadly. On a good day you had to be very careful. In storm conditions it was just about the most reckless thing a person could do.

Probably ten seconds passed. I was frozen as if in a dream.

This couldn't be happening, I thought, this could not be real.

I looked at the sky again. The storm would hit within ten minutes. I reckoned Rebecca would be right in the narrows under the cliffs when it did, about the most dangerous place possible.

I ran out of the house and along the beach back to the Derby stage where our dory with its outboard motor was tied up. I calmed down, forced myself to breathe evenly and took the seconds needed to check for gas (there was lots), ropes (I threw some in from the store), oars (they were in place), and a bailer and buoys (they were where they should have been). I knew the drill. The one cardinal rule I couldn't do anything about was to find a buddy to help or to tell someone what I was doing. There was absolutely no one around. Even old Johnny had disappeared. The whole Cove seemed deserted for that instant in time.

I jumped in the dory, pulled the engine's rip cord and I was gone, slow for a second or two and then full throttle as I headed in a straight line to Cook's Point.

By the time I gained on Rebecca an icy rain was falling. As I got close I could see she was pretty upset. But it was not about the storm, which still hadn't registered with her.

"How dare you," she yelled. "I can't even run away without a posse coming after me. Who do you think you are? You're driving that boat like a maniac." The wind had picked up and I had to strain to hear her.

My dory surged ahead of her rowboat. Once she turned sideways and looked at me, she saw the squall line and she twigged that we were about to be smacked by one hell of a storm.

In seconds we were drenched through to the skin and I was in danger of not being able to get close to her because of the heavy seas. I got one chance to throw her a rope and shout that I was going to tow her back up the harbor. My original plan of taking her around the point and into Cave Cove would have been suicidal once the storm was on us.

She was a true Newfoundlander, born and bred on the water. She knew exactly what trouble we were in and she grabbed that rope like her life depended on it.

It did.

She had difficulty tying a half hitch to the rowboat's apron in the pitching sea. It took a precious minute. I was praying to the Almighty again. I was in a bit of a pickle myself, because I couldn't take my hand off the idling motor to secure my rope. It was hard enough keeping the dory from crashing into the rowboat.

Rebecca signaled that she was ready. It was not perfect on my end but I couldn't piss away any more time. We had to go while we could still see the cliffs and the blur of bright greens, yellows and blues of the houses hugging our shoreline.

Cook's Cove was the only place in the harbor where there was a natural landing. I knew I had to pull away from the cliffs and stay in the middle of the harbor until I could see the government wharf off my stern. Instinct told me that only then could I turn toward our cove and the beach.

We pushed through the rain, battled the wind and scaled the waves in unison until I reckoned we were within one hundred yards of the wharf. I needed to aim us toward the little sandy beach beside the wharf and not think about having every bone in our bodies broken when we hit.

The boat and engine were being constantly swamped and my rope was coming loose. From somewhere I heard a scream and I was shocked to realize I was in the water. I surfaced to see that my boat was upside down and Rebecca was struggling to untie the rope connecting the boats before it got caught in

Seven for a Secret

the engine and she was dragged over too. I grabbed a buoy and used it as a floating pillow as I pitched up and down with the lops. Somehow I stayed near the rowboat. Rebecca was screaming at me and thank the Lord for small miracles, she reached for me with her long, strong arms. She pulled and I shoved and I went head first into the rowboat.

We each grabbed an oar and used them to keep the rowboat headed into the beach. We tried to make headway but for every inch forward, the swells pushed us back a yard, back out toward the narrows. Within ten minutes we had exhausted our strength. All we could do was sit in the middle of the rowboat, hang on with one hand and bail icy water with the other.

We heard the story of how we got rescued again and again for the rest of the summer. I knew I'd probably hear mangled versions of it for the rest of my life.

Nan, ever vigilant at our window, saw me take the dory. At first she kept rocking and rocking, faster and faster. Then Kate brought her a cup of tea and she could see Nan was agitated about something. Nan sloshed the tea and pushed Kate to the window. But all my cousin could see was a black storm raging over the harbor. Kate called to the twins for help and together the three of them soothed Nan and made her more comfortable. She hadn't spoken in that rocking chair for thirty years while she kept a vigil over the storms. She broke that silence with one word.

"Melinda," she said and pointed toward the harbor.

Kate understood. Somehow Melinda was out there on the water. Then Nan sat up straight and tall, told the children to be good and to stay put, ordered Kate to get waterproof gear for the both of them and they were out the door, stumbling down our lane, holding on to each other, Kate trying desperately hard to see through her tears and the torrential rain.

Nan told Kate to go to the Parks, the Childs, the Barneses and the Pumphreys and tell them she needed whatever men were home to go to the government wharf with ropes because someone needed help. Explain later, she ordered.

Nan gathered the Smiths, the Hickeys, the Mullens and the Lewises. And she went to the fish plant on the edge of the wharf to get my mom. No one thought of Aunt Grace scrubbing away in the church.

The men immediately organized a safety line on the wharf and everyone hung on to it as they talked about what was to be done.

My Matt came into the circle just as Nan was saying whoever went out on the water must wear lifejackets, be good swimmers and be very strong. No one wanted to tell my Matt who was in trouble but he figured it out. He told me later that he saw Kate and Nan and Mom and his first thought was that his Melinda must be sick to not be there helping out. Then he noticed, even in the slashing rain, that Kate was crying softly and that Mae was sobbing into Kate's shoulder.

He was the first volunteer. Chas and two other young fishermen quickly fell in behind him. Others, including Robert Gordon, offered to be in the next boat and the next boat, until however long it took to bring me in.

Then one of the Lewis men said he was pretty certain he could see something moving in the shadow behind the curtain of rain. Nan shook my mother and they tied themselves to the edge of the wharf and started shouting at the top of their lungs into the wind. Most people there hadn't heard my mom say a word above a whisper in a decade.

"Melinda, where are you…?Melinda…say something …Melinda."

It was my mom who heard me. "Over here, near the beach." It was all they needed to find us.

It was a desperate struggle. Me and Rebecca capsized and the men had to fish us out of the churning sea. I held on to that old buoy and Rebecca kept hold to my yellow skirt. We knew enough to stay together and we went with the big waves, didn't try to wrestle with them. I could hear my mom and Nan and I just knew we couldn't give up.

Arms finally dragged us aboard and honest to God, I don't remember nothing else except for the pounding on my chest, the horrible vomiting and the bone-chilling cold.

The biggest shock, of course, was when we came ashore and they saw that Rebecca was in the boat too.

CHAPTER EIGHT

◦

As deep as the grave

Within the hour the storm was over, the sun was tugging at the clouds and we were in bed at my house covered with blankets stacked as high as a fish flake. Rebecca wanted to be in her own bed but there was no one home and she was in no condition to argue. My mom got around to remembering that Grace was in the church and found her there scrubbing the pine floor quietly humming a hymn that praised Jesus the Savior. When she heard what had happened, she left the bucket in the middle of the aisle and came running up our lane. She wrapped Rebecca in her arms and only let her go to blow her nose and wipe the tears from the corners of her eyes. Rebecca didn't hug her mom back and kept telling Grace, none too kindly, that she was very tired and needed to sleep.

By dinnertime the relief had worn off and my Matt went back to his camp. He had come into the shelter of the harbor before the storm struck and he had to tend to his catch. While my mom was handing me my tenth cup of tea with another two heaping teaspoons of sugar, she gave me that look that said, how could the two of you have been so stupid as to go out for a boat ride with a storm coming on? I stalled for time and said I needed to sleep. I knew it wouldn't take her too long to find out that Dad's dory was missing.

I convinced Mom the danger was over so she could go back to work, or at least go down to the kitchen and bake some nice gooey toffee squares or make a big pan of chocolate fudge. Aunt Grace remembered her bucket left in the middle of the church and I shooed the kiddies off my bed but told them a bunch of wildflowers would be lovely. Kate settled in on the wooden chair by the window. I turned to Rebecca.

"So, my dearest cousin, what were you doing in the little rowboat? What did you mean when you said a girl can't even run away?"

Rebecca looked pretty glum but she told the truth. "My mom's been even more upset since I told her I wasn't going to camp. I figured you two would get out of it and I wasn't going alone. Dad is staying out of the house and only comes home to eat and sleep. Meals are pure agony. I have never seen her like this. I wanted to ask her about what happened when I was born but she's closed up, tighter than a clam. My chance of going to Boston was just slipping away. I could see she wasn't going to budge. I had to get out of the house. Just get away. I figured I could row to the cave."

She hesitated only a split second. "After I got to the cave, I thought I would walk overland to Frenchman's Bay and figure out a way to the States from there. There are always boats going down the coast. Once I got across the border I was going to get in touch with Mr. Harris. I saw on that letter in the pantry that his bank was on Boylston Street. He seemed such a nice man." Then she reached down and out of her bra she took a roll of soggy money. "I took all the bills from my savings tin. I figured once I was gone I wouldn't need it for teachers' college." She had a couple of hundred dollars, most of the money her dad paid her for her fish work. The only money she ever spent was on books about drawing and painting. What she had was enough to keep her going for a few weeks. I asked her, why today? Well, she said, the boat was just sitting there, it was a warm, sunny day, and she was alone. I asked if she had any regrets.

"Yes," she said. "If you had drowned, Melinda, I would have just slipped under the waves myself." Then she said that she was awfully tired and she soon fell asleep.

After supper Kate went out for a walk with Chas. Uncle Wilf came by, crushed Rebecca in a bear hug and practically carried her home. In the early evening my mom came in and lurked in the shadows. I knew trouble was looming. She was dusting my bureau with her apron.

"The Lewis boys found our dory, bottom up, about five miles out to sea. They towed it back. I think there is more to this than a couple of stupid girls going for a lark in a rowboat. Nan says she saw you get into the dory alone almost as the storm was starting. Now why would my daughter, a girl born and bred in the Cove, do that? Can you tell me the whole story, the true story, now?"

It had dawned on me by then that me and Rebecca could have drowned in that storm. And for what? I asked myself. Because my aunt was hiding something that kept Rebecca from going to Boston and that was making Rebecca so heartsick that she had tried to run away from the Cove. The first time anyone here had done that in our recorded history.

So I came right out and told Mom what Rebecca had done.

She sat down hard on my bed. Like me, she was astounded that Rebecca was hurting so bad that she had tried to leave all the pain behind. I reminded her that she had to take some of the blame, because she had promised to talk to Grace, and she hadn't done anything.

Then she admitted that she hadn't eaten in days, she was so sick to her stomach at the idea of confronting Grace. She just couldn't face it.

I didn't know what more to say. I thought back over the times I'd seen the two sisters together.

I racked my brains but couldn't come up with a single example of a time when I'd seen them at ease with each other or when Aunt Grace didn't boss us like she bossed everyone in the Cove.

I remembered when Daddy died. The only money we had was what was left in the sugar bowl in the pantry. By then Grace, being the midwife, knew that Mae was having twins. Grace wanted us to move in with them. She cleaned out the back room and made up it and the guest room for me, Mom and the babies. My mom argued that she would get a job and that she was perfectly able to look after her children on her own. One day when I came home from school she had all our belongings packed in boxes and she told me we were moving in with Nan. Mom's way of facing up to her sister was curious. I mean, we ended up moving out of our own place anyway.

Grace scrubbed the church by herself once every summer, she organized the Ladies' Aid committee to clean it every month and ordered the younger crowd to do it in between times. The garden party and time would have gone ahead every summer without a hitch if not one person had lifted a finger to give her a hand. She went out in the middle of the night whenever someone needed medical help and it was always her call if the sick person rested home or was put on board the ferry for the doctor or hospital. I'd never seen her toes tapping to jigs and reels. She loved her hymns, her piano and the church organ. But she played and sang with a furrow in her brow and a tight mouth like it was the biggest effort to make something nice. Despite her big house and having my sweet Uncle Wilf as a husband, she did not come across as a happy woman.

It was my mom who always had the kind word, the time to listen, the clean handkerchief to dry tears and the magic hand that could turn a cold day into a comfy sit by the stove. My mom was always on Aunt Grace's committees, but she didn't go to the meetings. If Grace was too much a tyrant, it was my mom who smoothed the waters. If Grace said no, it was my mom who turned it into a maybe. My Aunt Grace knew how to stand up in public and say thank you, knew how to write letters, how to set a good table, how to get us an extra visit from the medical boat, a new road. But it was my mom who made people work with a song in their hearts, made us all feel that we were good people.

The sisters were as different as an ocean and a lagoon. Yet they were family, and in the Cove, family was more important than anything.

Grace hated it when my mom went to work at the fish plant. She came to the house and reminded my mom that she was a Derby, not an ordinary fishwife. My mom smoked a few cigarettes and finally told Grace that she had to get ready for work. My mom was proud that she kept us off the welfare and independent, but all Grace could see was a widow woman refusing to accept her family's help.

Maybe I was asking too much of my mother. I felt pity for her. She tried to tell me I was in way over my head but I didn't hear it then. Somehow, in talking some more, she outwitted me. She got me to promise that I would go with her to see Aunt Grace about Rebecca. Was I foolish, or what!

The worst of it was that the waiting didn't end. The lobster run was one of the best we'd ever had and the canning section at the factory was running around the clock. My mom only came home to catch a couple of hours of sleep late at night and none of us saw her for another week.

We hung the new wallpaper in Flossie's room and turned it into a sun-kissed vale of roses. Once Mom got her oil heater, the room would be pretty and warm. My Matt was around a lot more. He said he didn't want me doing anything so harebrained again as go out in a boat alone. All this attention meant I was forever stumbling over Chas, too, because he just happened to be with my Matt whenever my Matt turned up our lane.

Rebecca had the toughest time of it. She had to stick to her story that she was going on a picnic and didn't see the squall line. We hardly saw her that next week because she was helping her dad with his lobster pots. The Christian Ladies' Prayer Camp was not mentioned again.

The boys came over on Saturday evening and we decided it was time we put the near-drowning behind us and celebrate being alive. Earlier in the summer Mom tried making this new drink called sarsaparilla. She set a row of big jars of the stuff out in the back porch. The dark, sticky syrup was squeezing through the tops and running down the sides and we figured that if we didn't drink it soon, it would explode. So I got down a couple of gallons of sarsaparilla and Nan put on a big pot of lobster chowder.

It was party time.

My Matt played the fiddle real good. He stood close to the open kitchen window so he could rest his beer on the sill. The guys wouldn't drink the sarsaparilla because it was sissy stuff, but us girls liked the rooty taste. Chas matched the fiddle with his accordion and it was not long before we were singing and clapping along.

The fiddle and squeezebox music escaped through the window, danced down the lane and soon word got around we were having a party, and Cove folks pushed into our big kitchen and spilled out into the dining room.

It was a good Newfie time. Lottie Kennedy was as big as a house. Her baby was due in a month's time, but she was there belting out country and western tunes and telling foolish stories over in the corner near the parlor door. Her husband, a man who liked his drink too much, went out back and got himself sloshed on moonshine.

Uncle Billy Dorry, who was no one's uncle, was playing the spoons. He was one of the old Cove bachelors so he was a fixture at all the parties. Always looked at the pretty girls but never touched. He brought along a couple of bottles of potato wine and a few of the boys were getting their first taste of the vile, potent moonshine. Good thing the next day was Sunday, 'cause they wouldn't be going fishing.

Mom, the lobster under control at the factory, was worrying if there was going to be enough chowder. I saw her borrowing smokes from Uncle Billy and tapping her toes in time to "Chickens in the Shavings." With a glass of Nan's partridgeberry wine in her hand, she was holding her sides laughing as she listened to Lottie telling the old jokes about Newfies going down the road looking for work in the big cities.

"How many Newfies fit in a Ford Falcon?" she shouted out.

"Twenty—just tell them it's going to Toronto."

Juanita Barnes was sitting on Young Charlie Mullen's lap. Looking at things I'd say my Matt and me might have trouble getting down the aisle before them. And Juanita was a year behind me in school. Her mom had youngsters in diapers.

Charlie had a share in the *Irene L.*, the ferryboat named after his mother, and he was a good fisherman besides. All the Mullens were good with motors and could fix anything. Juanita could mimic all the Hank Snow tunes. She learned them just hearing them once on the radio.

Millie Pumphrey and Annie Lake were sitting in the dining room having a good jag about washing and babies. I saw more than a couple of glasses of wine pass through their hands. Robert Gordon came by. He brought a case of beer from the bootlegger's. He stood apart from the young crowd, his flannels pressed and his cotton shirt like it was out of the package. His hair was Brylcreemed and he was freshly shaved. He looked at no one except Rebecca

The laughter was reaching Rebecca's eyes as she kicked up her heels, going faster and faster to keep up with the rhythm. She was dressed in khaki capri pants and a white blouse with her thick braid tossing every which way. A couple of young fellas were flirting with her and I was a little shocked to see that she was giving them just as good back. I looked a little closer and noticed she was wearing a deep pink lipstick and, the shame of it, the second button on her blouse was undone. No wonder Robert kept his eye on her.

Chas and my Matt were grinning from ear to ear as their fingers moved quick as seal flippers in the water. They had been playing together since they were youngsters so they could lead and follow each other like they were out walking, and that was a big part of the fun.

Georgie and Flossie went under the table to eat a bag of cherries. Their fingers and mouths were stained red with the juice. One of Chas's father's supply boats had come into the Cove earlier in the day, and as a special favor the captain had saved a couple of crates of the juicy fresh cherries for the Cove. Chas brought along the best ones to the party. I had never tasted a fresh cherry before and Chas and my Matt had a good laugh as the juice ran down my chin and I almost choked on the pit. They were some good. I must have eaten a pound. I wondered if people in Boston got to eat wonderful things like cherries all the time.

Mabel Smith came in the door. She never came to a party with a date but always left leaning on some drunken fella's arm. I saw her take more than a nip or two when the boys handed around the potato wine. Her canary-yellow blouse was enough to make me dizzy and her shorts were way too tight to be decent. We were sure as hell not left wondering what cut of knickers she was wearing. She was putting on weight. She brought a box of bologna sandwiches, not something I would bring to a party but the guys were wolfing them down.

Lord dyin', that was when Pauline Pumphrey walked in. Her mom, Millie, was the biggest gossip, but Pauline's training was going real well. Both of them together brought to mind that old saying: A woman's tongue is her sword, and she does not let it rest. Pauline had been telling people I was pregnant and tried to commit suicide by going to sea in a squall. I could have pushed her bony nose right into her round face. I straightened up when she was looking my way to show her my flat stomach. There was another saying here that makes it hard to fight malicious tongues like Pauline's: Where there's smoke, there's fire. She was an old maid, twenty-one years old, not married and no prospects on the horizon. She was all right to look at if you could get past the hoser of a nose. There was no doubt that someone would come along sooner or later though. Every woman got married in the Cove or else went off somewhere to hide her shame.

I saw the corner of my mother's dress as she put her leg over someone sitting on the floor to get in the pantry. She came out carrying a tray of clean tumblers. I wondered why she hadn't married again. She was faded and tired but even with touches of gray she was still pretty and only thirty-four years old. She wouldn't be so tired if she had someone helping her fix the roof and pay the bills. My dad had been dead five years and as far as I knew she hadn't had a date in that time. She must miss him some bad, I thought.

Kate came to sit on the table with me. She would never say it but she wanted to be close to Chas especially since Mabel walked in and latched on to every male over fourteen by simply batting her heavily mascaraed eyelashes.

The boys struck up a real fast one— "We'll rant and we'll roar like true Newfoundlanders." The air was stuffy and the kitchen was jam packed.

"I'm dizzy," Kate said as she tried to pick up the rhythm with her hands.

Funny she mentioned it at that moment. I was having a grand time and then all of a sudden it was as though the table had a mind of its own and it wanted me off. I saw Mom helping Juanita to a chair and pushing her head down between her legs. Rebecca was sitting on the floor next to the open door looking totally glazed.

My mom made her way across the room.

"Surely you girls haven't been drinking the beer or potato wine?" she asked. Kate shook her head. Nan came in with another bottle of sarsaparilla. She started to open it and at the same instant, the top blew off and hit the ceiling with a thud. Everyone in the house froze. Even the music stopped.

"What have you got there, Nan Derby? Sounds pretty potent. Can I have a little glass?" asked Uncle Billy Dorry while everyone had a good laugh at Nan's total consternation.

It didn't take my mom long to twig to the problem. She thought she had made a soft drink suitable for young ladies.

This one had a definite kick and us young ladies had been knocking it back all evening. No wonder the table was swaying under me.

Mom rescued us all by noticing that it was almost midnight. The party was over the second the clock struck Sunday. There was a scramble among the fellas to see who could stand up and then, among those who could walk, who would walk Mabel to her door (and further, none of us doubted).

I think my Matt wanted me to go to the door with him for a goodnight kiss and cuddle but I couldn't tell 'cause I couldn't see very well and I couldn't stand up anyway. Rebecca was two sheets to the wind and sitting on the floor and Kate was throwing up through the window.

Best party all summer.

CHAPTER NINE

❧

Pigs may fly, but they are very unlikely birds

It wasn't so great on Sunday morning. The church bells were ringing in my head and Kate was still throwing up her guts. I begged Mom to let me stay put in my bed this one Sunday. Because she felt a little guilty she let us miss church. Nan came in later with a cup of milky tea but neither me nor Kate could look at it. I went over the edge when I saw the milk swirling round and round. Kate crawled further under her pillow and moaned something pitiful.

Later I asked Nan if Rebecca was at church and she said no. Grace said Rebecca was flushed and feverish with a summer cold. My nan didn't have the nerve to suggest what Rebecca's real complaint might be. She said our friend Mr. Gordon was a real hero and when he left our place he was practically carrying Rebecca home, step by step.

Rebecca told us she had to crawl up our lane to come see us that afternoon. Kate and I were close to normal by then, but Rebecca really liked the root flavor of the sarsaparilla and she'd been close to the pantry so she'd drunk a tumblerful every time she stopped dancing to catch her breath. By that time we were laughing about it and wondering what Pauline Pumphrey was telling everyone. She had it all over the Cove already that we were getting high and mighty this summer. You couldn't stop her tongue from wagging so the best thing you could do was laugh.

We were lolling on the green chesterfield in the front parlor when Nan came in to tell us we could rest some more, that supper was cold roast beef and potato salad and it would be ready in half an hour. Just as she turned to leave, Rebecca leaned over to fix her shoe and the gold ring fell out of her blouse. It was small and not many people would even notice it but Nan did.

Her eyes fixed on the ring. Her mouth was working but nothing came out. Pretty soon there were tears coming down her cheeks and she was fumbling for a hankie in her apron pocket. We begged her to tell us what was the matter but she just cried some more.

We didn't have a clue what to do. Finally, after a few hiccups, she reached out to hold the ring and was able to talk.

"This ring was handmade by Grandpappy for our youngest son, Edward. The white stone is not a stone at all, but Edward's tooth, one he lost in a fall. The band is real gold. Grandpappy brought it back from a trip to the States. Some fella gave him gold to pay for a load of fish. He changed the gold to Newfoundland money except for this small piece he brought home to show me. Joe hammered away at it to see if he could make a ring for me but there wasn't enough metal. We decided on a ring for baby Edward just when his tooth was knocked out. I got the idea of putting the tooth in the ring.

"Edward was the most beautiful baby in the world and he loved the ring. He understood right away that he had to take good care of it and it was never out of his sight."

"What happened?" I asked, and both Kate and Rebecca gave me a swift kick.

We pieced together the story in between the sniffles. Edward was a little boy when his daddy died and Herb went into the city to find work and Grace was helping out on the flakes. The man Nan had been helping make fish got married within the year and his wife took over Nan's job. Nan had to find something else to do to bring in cash. She became the first woman in the Cove to start a business. She worked morning to night making rugs and bed quilts in fancy patterns that she sold to a merchant in St. John's who had been a friend of Grandpappy's.

The handwork was so well liked that she kept getting telegrams for more orders. One autumn night during a terrible storm she was so intent on finishing a rug she didn't notice that Edward wasn't in his bed. Somehow he got out of the house. (She was bawling her eyes out by this time and Mom had quietly come into the parlor.) Some said he must have fallen into the harbor or wandered into the woods and was blinded by the rain and wind and froze to death. His little body was never found.

"I always believed that he was found far away and was living with another family, and that someday he would walk in and I would know him because he'd have that ring to show me."

By this time we were all bawling. Mom had come in and put her arms around Nan and was telling her she didn't have to dredge up all this old pain. But Nan said, no, it was time she dealt with it. She wanted to know exactly how we found the ring. It was washed up in a tangle of seaweed near our cave, we told her. Rebecca saw the shine of the gold and it took us a few minutes to get it because it was caught in a fish bone. We called it lucky because Rebecca did real good in her maths when she wore it writing the provincial exams. She couldn't remember an equation and when she absentmindedly rubbed the ring, the equation came back to her. It happened again and again. And no one had to remind Nan that Rebecca was wearing the ring when she went out in the storm.

Rebecca put the ring in the palm of Nan's hand and pushed her fingers closed around it. "You must keep it and put it somewhere safe, Nan."

But Nan was not finished. She looked my mom in the eye and said there were a couple of other things she had to explain. She said seeing Melinda get in the dory last week and being able to alert the men in the Cove of the trouble meant that her years of sitting out storms were not in vain. She said she always waited because she felt Edward would come back in a storm, the way he left.

"But that's past now and in future I won't be a nuisance whenever there is a blow coming. I'll just go about my chores." We assured her over and over that she had never been a nuisance.

"I've been waiting for Edward all these years. I forbade my daughters to mention his name. I know now he won't be coming home and I accept that. I thank the Lord that Melinda and Rebecca are with us today because I was watching for my boy. My one regret is that the only photo I had of my precious Edward was lost in a fire."

Nan and Mom were crying into each other's shoulder. I couldn't tell who was in whose arms. By this time we were all drenched with tears and the cold supper was a warm blob out in the hot kitchen.

While chomping back on the hunks of beef and the salad I remembered where I had seen that photo with its blackened edges. I caught my cousins' eyes. They remembered too. One secret told.

CHAPTER TEN

-❧-

Wait a fair wind and you'll get one

Monday was washday. There was always a rush to be first with drying on the line. You had to have it out by nine or be the talk of the Cove for laziness. Some biddies, Annie Lake to name one, rose from their cozy beds before dawn to stoke their stoves to have hot water when first light came. Then they would go around the rest of the week simpering and letting it slip every chance they got that they couldn't understand why everyone was so late with their washing this week and add sweetly, "Idle hands make idle minds." We resisted the temptation to bat them over the head with a rolling pin.

Nan and I worked like slaves to make the nine o'clock deadline and not put our house to shame. When Kate was here she hung the clothes on the line across our back field. The arthritis in Nan's shoulders made it hard for her to bend over the tubs and we were a little slow. So having Kate do the hanging job suited me just fine. The loss of face of coming in close to last made me stay indoors and hide.

There's nothing prettier than a line of crisp, white laundry sucking the freshness from a gentle breeze. And to sleep between sheets dried by a sea breeze is close to mortal bliss.

I was taking in the first line of dried sheets, thinking about how I might be sharing the thrill of fresh sheets with my Matt within the year, when my mom walked into the kitchen. She was off early. The lobster was all canned or shipped away whole, so the foreman told her to go home and get some sleep because the salmon would be ready for canning in a couple of days. She grabbed a cigarette from the pack in the warming oven above the stove, did not notice that at least three were missing, and sat tapping her fingers against the wooden table. Something was on her mind.

"I'm not tired enough to go to bed right away so I think, seeing as how you're finished with the washing, that you and I should go and pay your Aunt Grace a visit. She should be finishing up her wash by now too," she said.

She had that glint in her eye and I knew she meant business. Kate was there to baby-sit the rest of the wash so I had no excuses. I took my time finding a sweater but it was no use stalling. My mom was ready.

Just as Mom thought, Aunt Grace was cleaning up after the Monday wash. She was surprised to see us on a Monday morning and we were surprised that Rebecca was nowhere to be seen because the wash was one of her main jobs. Mom explained that she got off early from the plant for a hard-earned rest. We sat on the day bed waiting for Aunt Grace to finish mopping the floor. I wasn't sure that my mom had it in her, but as soon as Grace put down the mop, my mom asked her if we could go into the parlor to have a talk.

Aunt Grace still took her time. She got down a bottle of white cream from a high shelf in the pantry and lathered it between her fingers and halfway up her arms. I'd seen her do this a thousand times, probably the only woman over eighteen in the Cove who took care of her skin. Of course she had to take off her apron and run a comb through her hair. We were going into the parlor, you see. Before she started her grooming, she'd put the kettle on the burner and as she finished, it whistled for her to come and make the tea. She did up a tray with the Wedgwood teapot, china cups, silver spoons, linen napkins and almond shortbread cookies, another one of her specialities. Finally, she lifted the tray and beckoned for us to follow her into the parlor.

By this time both of us had lost our nerve. We sat down and neither of us knew where to put our eyes. I looked at the photos and Mom was fascinated by the painting over the piano, the one of the little stream running into the sea. Aunt Grace poured the tea, cleared her throat and she startled us by opening the talk.

"If you're here about raffling off another cushion this summer, it's too late. The Ladies' Aid had a meeting yesterday and we've decided on a card party."

"Why, no, Grace. That's not why we're here. There's something Melinda wants to tell you," said my mom.

Well, of all the mean tricks. I had to think fast.

"It's about Rebecca," I said, "and the boating accident. You see, Aunt Grace, I want to tell you what really happened. Rebecca keeps saying she was going on a picnic. The truth is she was so upset she was trying to run away. She wanted to leave Cook's Cove so bad she was going to row to Cave Cove and walk overland to Frenchman's Bay and catch a fishing boat going to the States. She had all her money on her." My mom gave me a dirty look that said, *Get to the point, we haven't got all day.* "She wanted to go to Boston so bad that she decided to go by herself. She had it all planned out. She even knew how to find that Mr. Harris."

"I don't believe you, Melinda. You've told me tales before

and I have no reason to believe that Rebecca would want to leave the Cove. She would never leave her father. She doesn't want to learn about art. She wants to go to teachers' college and then come back here and teach. She's been saying so since her first day at school. I know my daughter a lot better than you do."

"Maybe you should check the tin can where she's been keeping her money all these years. I bet you'll find that it's empty," I said. It was worth a try. I had no idea if Rebecca had put the money back. Still, I was no match for my aunt.

"I would never open Rebecca's money tin and if I did, there could be many reasons why Rebecca would have moved her savings.

"But I am glad that you came with your mother today because I want to go over this only one more time, young lady. Rebecca is not going to Boston, or anywhere else, until she sets off to teachers' college in St. John's next year. Is that clear?"

Well, she got me madder than a hatter. The old vixen didn't miss a chance to show us that she was in charge and none of us could do a thing about it. I looked calm but I was blowing my top and Mom was looking scared as she saw my nostrils flare and my eyebrows go straight out.

I lit into my aunt. "I know why you won't let Rebecca go off the island. So does Rebecca, and for that matter, Kate knows the secret too, and my mom," I spat out. "We came today to ask you to talk to Rebecca about why you changed her birth date. That might patch things up between you two. She's old enough to be told whatever the story is. If you were concerned that we'd find out about it, we already know, so there's nothing to lose and nothing to hide. She can go into Corner Brook to see about any papers she might need. If we all know the big secret and no one else can find out, why not let her go to art school? She has real talent, Mr. Harris says so."

She just sat there, real silent, with her back stiff and her lips tight. I started to get frightened. I wondered if I'd gone too far.

Aunt Grace turned ever so slowly and spoke to my mother. "You're part of this, Mae. I can't believe my own sister would turn on me. Not after everything I've done for you."

Trust my mom to ruin everything. She started to cry. "I didn't turn on you, Grace. The girls found out by themselves. Melinda told me about searching for Rebecca's birth certificate and finding it in a box. They thought you would change your mind about the trip to the States and they wanted to be all ready to go. I told her she had to tell you. That's why I brought her here. Grace, think about it, Rebecca almost drowned, that's how desperate she was. You can't let this pass.

"You told me years ago that Rebecca was a little early, that night she almost died of fever, but I never told a soul, not even Nan. You told me in secrecy and I kept that secret. What the girls did was wrong, they should not have gone through private papers, but we can't change the fact that they know that Rebecca was born much earlier than you told me.

"Please, Grace," she went on, "don't be so hard on Rebecca. She's a troubled young lady, and no one is explaining anything to her. She needs her mother to help her, not keep her back."

Wow, that was a big speech for my mother. But to Grace we were just chicken liver. "I can't abide disrespect or disobedience from my daughter or from my nieces for that matter. Surely you're not telling me that these girls went through my papers? That's impossible. What's this nonsense about seeing proof of her age? There's absolutely no way for you to prove anything about Rebecca's birth."

Now I never expected her to take that line. She was acting like she hadn't heard a word we had said. The nerve!

"There was no reason for the girls to lie to me, Grace," my mom said very quietly.

"Well, it's not the first time they haven't told the truth but this time they've gone too far. I can't believe that you even listened to them, Mae. And I'll certainly not repeat that mistake. Good day to the both of you." With that she stood up straight and tall, picked up the half-empty cups, put them back on her tray and left us sitting in the parlor.

Mom mumbled something about needing to get some sleep as she pulled me out of the room and out the side door. I didn't remind her that we hadn't got around to confronting Aunt Grace about Rebecca being an American or the father's name on her birth certificate.

Aunt Grace obviously didn't have a clue that I had borrowed the certificate and it was hidden in my bottom drawer.

I wasn't a quitter but I was dead tired of it all. I wanted to shove the whole mess under a bed and bury it under the dust ruffle.

Walking up the road I wondered why Rebecca hadn't been there to help her mom on washday. Soon I was to find out that my cousin was no longer the perfect daughter, that she had tossed her princess crown to the bottom of the sea.

A couple of nights later I had a horrible nightmare. All the folks were saying that the Cove was no place for an American bastard. I was vicious about it but my tongue was caught in a metal trap and I couldn't say a word. I struggled to come out of it and as the dawn light seeped into my room, Kate, who is as blind as a bat without her glasses, was almost in my face as she tried to see what I was up to.

"I was just going to get a bucket of water to put you out

of your misery. We'd better get the chores done if we're going to that baby shower for Lottie Kennedy," she said.

To folks in the Cove trouble was an everyday thing. A lost net, a poor catch, a sore back, a dull day for the wash, frozen water pipes, a dried-up well, a hand cut to the bone while splitting the fish, no work, not enough work, too much work, a broken heart, no money, not enough money, bad fish, too much fish, wind, a leaky roof, a broken chimney, a gassy stomach, a broken engine, boils on the neck, a son who doesn't want to fish, fog, no sugar at the shop until the boat comes in next week, no more credit from Eaton's, a wood-stove that won't light, men back late from the fishing grounds, no dole, a missing tooth, a missing son. There was no end to it. Everyone had troubles.

For a girl of fifteen, trouble meant *in trouble*—expecting, in the family way, in a delicate condition, sick. Lottie had been *in trouble* but her man did the right thing and walked her down the aisle in the spring. He was a jerk but he took away her trouble and made her a married woman so we could all visit and go goo goo over the little jackets, nappies and sleepers.

Rebecca came by and we went to my room to doll up for Lottie's baby shower. There was no talk of family secrets as Rebecca used too much of my powder and lipstick. Even Kate was quieter than usual. She too dabbed on a little Frosty Pink lipstick while Rebecca and I raised eyebrows over her shoulder. I found it strange, even then, that we weren't chattering like old times. The quiet made me nervous and I put on so much Evening in Paris that a mist of it floated down the stairs with me.

The shower was an afternoon of cards—auction was the game of choice—and toss-the-ring and having a good time listening to Lottie go on about how she was planning to have at least a dozen kids. The way I looked at it she probably would, too, because her husband, Jamie, was a mean son-of-a-bitch who liked his drink and when he was drinking he liked to give the orders and be the big man in the Cove. He rushed every girl in the harbor and then young Lottie started her period and put on a bra and he was her first date. And her with no mother to steer her clear of trouble. Once she was "in love" no one could tell her that Jamie was a rat. So there we were putting the best face on a bad situation. We knew how to do that with bells on.

The shower talk turned to Princess Margaret's wedding gown. Juanita Barnes was passing around a bit cut out of the *Western Bay* newspaper that her cousin sent in the mail. Some fashion people in Toronto were copying the heavy white brocade dress and selling it for a hundred and twenty bucks. Still a sight more than the lace and rayon taffeta in the catalogue for thirty-seven fifty, and you could pay Eaton's on the instalment plan, four dollars a month. Not that I had been looking at bridal gowns. Not me.

That talk went nowhere fast when we remembered that it was Lottie's party and Lottie couldn't fit into a wedding dress by the time her Jamie was convinced to do the right thing and marry her. He'd been shooting off at the mouth about not having to buy the cow since he was getting the milk for free. Lottie went around with her eyes cast to the ground like a fallen woman. Some of us girls talked to some of our boys and one night they took Jamie out for a real boozer. Around three in the morning they hammered on Aunt Grace's door and Jamie, with his buddies holding him up, told her he wanted to order up the minister for a wedding. Aunt Grace appraised the situation right away, got a piece of paper, wrote out Jamie's intentions, and got him to sign. The wedding was put together around him, the boys made sure he showed up, and he was a married man.

No catch though. Lottie was respectable but she would have a tough life ahead of her. But any husband was better than no husband. At least Lottie would one day get her own little house, a pretty garden, and soon enough she would have a beautiful baby to take her mind off her troubles.

Sally Lewis was telling Lottie to be careful of fevers because she'd heard that four children in Newfoundland had died from polio in May and June. This got Sally going. She was born healthy twenty years ago but got sick on a whim whenever she wanted some attention. A sore throat meant we had to listen to a half-hour of horror, a headache was sure to be a brain tumor, a cough was TB, and a jammed fart sent her right to the Western Memorial Hospital in Corner Brook.

"Did you hear," said Sally, "my uncle, Jimmy, has heart trouble. He'll die before the winter is out, that's for certain. And my granddad has taken to his bed again with a summer cold. It is sure to turn to pneumonia. It always does in our family. And my cousin Jane had a D. and C. last week because she was bleeding so bad. You should be careful, Lottie, when you have that baby. Women still die from childbirth, you know. I shouldn't be eating these sweets. They give me terrible indigestion and I'll be farting all night."

Well, with that, none of us knew where to look. Bless her heart but Lottie jumped in and saved the moment by saying she was hoping to have the baby in the city. She was due in a little over two weeks' time and she'd heard the road would be unofficially opened by then. If it was she would get a drive in and stay with some cousins and wait there for the pains to begin. She had it in her head to be the first Cove woman to have a baby the modern way, in the hospital.

"Everyone will be having their babies in the hospital once the road is done," she said.

That turned the talk to the new road.

"I'm outta here as soon as I can buy me a car and load her up," said Mabel Smith. She'd been saying that since they blasted the first rocks in the spring. None of us doubted her for a minute. Her mom and dad would look after her little boy and with her beauty school training she wouldn't have trouble getting a job. There was nothing for Mabel in the Cove. She was used goods, got pregnant three summers ago while doing her hairdressing training at the vocational school in the city. The guy wouldn't marry her and she came home with little Jimmy. She drank too much and some folks thought she ran around with too many fellas. The Cove was no good for a nineteen-year-old unmarried mother who wouldn't stay out of sight. Her mom and dad already treated Jimmy like a son and when she was gone, he would forget her soon enough. It wasn't so uncommon around here.

Sally went back to her aches and pains. "We'll be able to go to the hospital in under an hour on the road instead of waiting for the ferry and then doing it in two hours, if the weather holds. I'm sick and tired of having the wind and rain decide if someone should live or die."

She was always a little melodramatic but this time she was right. My Matt's little brother might not have died if the storm hadn't slowed down the boat.

"It's the electricity I want," I said. "They're putting up the poles as they come through with the road. Frenchman's Bay already has lights. Mom says she'll buy one of those electric toasters in the catalogue."

It was then that Kate chimed in with her two cents' worth. "It also means that anyone can come out here and drive up and down the road and gawk. Youngsters will be asking to go in the city to shop and to go to the movies. No one will be happy any more sitting around listening to a good yarn or dancing up a storm to fiddle music when you can put a record on the hi-fi."

What could we say? We wanted the road so we could put a record on the hi-fi and go shopping in Corner Brook. City girls didn't understand.

I suggested we open the gifts. Lottie was a child herself as she unwrapped the tiny bibs, the flannelette diapers, the packets of safety pins, the Johnsons' powder, the white nighties, and even the big box of Kotex someone put in to torment. She was so easy to please. The baby would be four months old before she turned fifteen. Her mother died having her. Her dad never got over his wife leaving him with a baby and Lottie practically grew up on her own. She was so happy during her wedding we all gave Jamie another look-over.

The potted meat sandwiches were small and dainty but the date squares and cream puffs made it a fair spread. Mrs. Kennedy, who was giving Lottie the shower, looked concerned I was going to eat the whole plate of squares. I had more manners than that but the look reminded me to hand around the platters. The Kennedys were another of Lottie's burdens. Her mother-in-law liked the gin and Lottie had taken over rearing up Jamie's six young brothers and sisters. Old man Kennedy liked his beer, had a bad temper like his son, and money was always scarce with that crowd.

I had to leave off worrying about Lottie when I heard Mabel Smith asking Kate if she liked the Cove better this summer. Kate acted like she didn't know that was a loaded question.

"I've always liked it here," she said. "The weather has been a little better this year." And with that she got up and came over for a cream puff. Not bad. I knew she was sneaking off almost every night to see Chas, and folks were beginning to ask where he was all the time.

Mabel decided Rebecca was better game.

"I hear you and old man Gordon are mooning over each other," she said.

I expected a rapid-fire denial, but Rebecca shocked me so much I almost choked on my date square.

"He hasn't asked me to marry him yet if that's what you're asking," Rebecca said with a brazen look. This was news to me. I hadn't seen much of her since the boating accident and while I knew she was mad at her mom, I thought she was spending more time with her dad.

It was a strange summer. My Matt was around keeping an eye on me. Kate was off somewhere with Chas most of the time and Rebecca didn't want anything to do with us. We were all going down different paths, slipping away from each other.

I heard Mabel laugh and say to Rebecca, "I can help you look a little more grown up if you want to snag a husband."

And to that my dear cousin replied, "Maybe you should come over to my place one night. We could have a good talk." That got me right in the ribs. Rebecca always came to me if she wanted help or advice. I'd always been her older sassy cousin (at least I thought I was) who knew a few things about life and could make her laugh.

Then another conversation started up. It was between Mabel and Lottie. They were talking about bedroom stuff. Now this got my attention.

"You're going to have to get your Jamie to use one of those French safes when he gets the urge. One small baby is enough to take care of. And you have the other six to look after too," said Mabel.

The room had gone real quiet. We stayed silent, hoping to learn anything that would help us when our boys wanted more than a kiss and a feel.

"A girl has to put her foot down and that's all there is to it," said Mabel. "And if you do get caught, there's still things you can do. You don't have to have a dozen kids underfoot." Lottie hung her head, her shoulders sagged. Her baby bump suddenly looked much too big for her tiny body.

"I got my nerve up one time to hint at one of those things for when after the baby is born, and he got all mad and said married people don't use stuff like that and he didn't want to hear no more talk about it," said Lottie.

I knew then why Mabel didn't have another baby. She was often seen down in the fishermen's shacks after dark. I knew too that Lottie was doomed to a life of eternal pregnancies unless Jamie fell overboard some morning when he went fishing dead drunk.

Not for me, that life. So I paid attention to these "French safes." I wondered if they were the same thing as a French letter I heard the boys snickering about a while back. I would ask my Matt. Juanita Barnes was paying real close attention too. She and Charlie Mullen had been going steady all summer. And, heavens, Kate was listening too.

Then the chairs were being pushed back. In the long silence after Mabel and Lottie's talk, Rebecca was able to say that she had to be getting along home to get supper for her dad. We trooped along the Cove road like noisy bluejays, like we used to. The sun was shining, the wind was calm and Kate and Rebecca were by my side.

CHAPTER ELEVEN

❧

Lonesome as a gull on a rock

After the baby shower I stayed away from Rebecca. I didn't like the way my cousin was changing. If Rebecca wanted that hussy for a best friend, that was her business. My cousin knew where to find me. And Aunt Grace was going to be off limits for a long time.

Instead, I decided to go after my mom about a fall wedding. I was not in trouble but it was only a matter of time. My Matt was keen to explore all of me and I was pretty interested in him. He had been popping in for visits at the oddest times since the rescue and was putting on his lonesome eyes.

The following Monday night I found Mom sitting at the kitchen table and staring into space. She didn't look in the mood to talk about marriage. Her back was too straight and her fingers were locked around her cigarette with a hint of white knuckle. The long shifts down at the plant were getting to her.

My mom took all the work that came her way. She said she couldn't go through another winter with us all sleeping in the dining room. But she looked so tired and washed out. Her hands were a mess, flecked with bruises, nicks, swollen veins and broken skin and nails. Her shoulders were stooped. Dried fish scales stuck to her skirt and shabby blouse. And she was so skinny. I could tell she had enough troubles. So when my Matt came by with Chas tagging along behind him like a puppy dog, the four of us decided to go for a walk over to our half-finished house.

My Matt worked his skin to the bone with his dad because in the spring he was determined to work his own boat instead of having a half-share in his dad's. You see, married men had their own boats.

The fishing stopped after the herring in November and he would be off in the woods cutting timber for the paper mill in Corner Brook. Last winter he was done in the woods early because a tree fell the wrong way and he was pinned underneath. I thought I would be nursing him a while, but as soon as he was up and about he took a job out at the lighthouse on Wee Ball, monitoring weather patterns for some research project at the university. I showed him how to do the math and then he was gone for two months. When he came back this spring I hardly saw him at all because he got a job blasting rocks for the new road. They were building the road from two directions, toward us from the city and then a five-mile stretch at the back of Cook's Point. The two ends would meet near Cook's Point where they were blasting through the rock. The fishing was a poor living without a winter job that paid hard cash. The fool saved every penny for his new boat and fishing license and our house.

I felt forlorn without my Matt. Kate kept me away from trouble, but she was not my Matt. It was a real treat seeing more of him this summer, especially on a Monday night.

"Did your dory sink?" I cracked.

He linked my arm. He was a man of few words.

"No, my love, but for the first time this summer, the bait is ready for tomorrow so here I am, ready for a night of loving."

I looked back to see if Kate and Chas heard this foolish talk. They were back along the road discussing politics and books. If I heard the name Joey Smallwood one more time, I swore I would scream. Wasting a perfectly beautiful summer evening, if you asked me. I could see that they were no longer coming our way but had headed down to the beach.

My Matt was pretty determined to get me into a dark corner. I could feel the strength in him easing into me and he practically pulled me along the path to our house. Or at least the shell of our house. The bridge to the side door was a broad plank resting on a pile of rocks. He helped me jump up into the kitchen. There was enough light to see where the sink would be. We had to be careful because the two-by-fours were full of splinters and there were nails, sawdust and bits of lumber everywhere. The house was framed in and I could walk into the living room and see where the big picture window and front door would be, see where the plumbing would be for the bathtub and toilet in the indoor bathroom and go down the short hall to the three bedrooms. The plans called the biggest empty space the Master Bedroom, and this was where my Matt led me.

"Melinda, my girl, I want to keep you in this room forever," he whispered.

We moved to a dark corner, the one furthest away from the lane, the one closest to the lapping waters of the cove.

Then we were on the floor and he was tugging at my blouse. There were no secret places between us. I knew exactly what he wanted, and he knew exactly what he was not getting. I gave in on the bra last summer. He unhooked the eyes in one expert move and I opened his shirt so I could rest my breasts on his naked chest. He was so warm and it felt so good. He was anxious to suck and I knelt up so he could get a good mouthful. I had missed him so much that I ground into him. He went after the curve of my neck and sucked and bit so hard I gasped.

It was not long before he wanted me to suck him too. He pushed my head down to his zipper and I couldn't tell who missed who the most.

Later, we smoked in the darkness, our bodies curved into each other. My Matt kept an old blanket rolled in a corner and we spread it over ourselves. Even a July night could get chilly when you're alongside mountains and the Atlantic. I was very content but my Matt was not.

"Melinda, my maid, I want to go to bed with you at night and I want to wake up with you in the morning. I want you, not my mother, making my breakfast and packing my lunch and having my supper on the table. When is this nonsense going to end? It looks like you're not going away, so why can't we just get hitched?"

He was tearing my heart out. Had I really been thinking of going off to Boston and leaving this true-heart behind? Was I mad to have been thinking about going to nursing school? Now I asked myself, truly, what was I waiting for? Did it matter if we were married this October, this spring, or next summer? What odds if I finished school? I could get breakfast on the table and have beautiful babies without a high school diploma.

I changed the subject. "What's a French safe? Is it the same as a French letter?" I asked. I could feel him laughing.

"Where did you pick up that gutter language and what's this about?"

"I want to know. I hate it when I don't know. Mabel Smith

was talking about them at the baby shower the other day."

"Matter of fact, they are the same thing and I have one here in my pocket if you want to see." With that he took out of a package a greasy bit of rubber rolled up in a plastic ring that wasn't bigger than a half-dollar.

"Well?" I asked. I'd made a fool of myself already so I thought I might as well learn something.

He was laughing even harder as he gently showed me how the rubber unwound, see, and, well, it meant that the girl wouldn't have a baby.

I saw the sense of it right away. "You mean, if we use one of these things, I won't get caught?" For once in my lifetime I was shy and I snuggled into my Matt. "Do you want to marry a virgin, love?"

There was a moment of silence as he took a deep draw on his cigarette.

"Let's just say I want to marry you." I heard the honesty and the hunger in his raspy voice.

He dropped the cigarette and drew me to him with a deep French kiss. I heard the thrust of the tide coming in over the rocks on the beach and I felt his need. My own body answered and I helped him out of his corduroys while he helped me take off my step-ins. It was the first time we'd been all skin-to-skin and it was truly the most delicious thing that had ever happened to me. He fiddled with the French thing and I arched to meet his first thrust.

I ached with the joy of it. My Matt and I were one, a togetherness I never thought possible. I clung and moved with him. I wanted to lick every inch of his skin. I never wanted it to stop. I wanted to grab his hair and force him to kiss me until we ate each other alive.

I felt the miracle of the final urgency and he rolled off me.

I was pretty sure there should be something else but I was

so heady with the wonder of our togetherness that I let it go. This time.

"Jesus," he said with a touch of real concern. "The thing broke. I've had it in my wallet for a couple of years."

I was in a bit of a daze and my brain was woolly. I couldn't worry about it now.

A little later, my Matt woke me up. He had to go fishing and his dad would be wondering where he was. I came back to this world and I felt him pushing a ring on my finger.

"We are engaged now, my love."

I thought of my mother, held him close and told him I'd wear the ring around my neck. That it would be our secret until I could talk my mom around. I would talk to her real soon, I said. I dressed and ran along the road, across the potato patch, through the back door and up the back stairs. I was in bed at the count of three but not soon enough.

"What's that funny smell coming off you?" whispered Kate.

"I came home through the potato field. Go to sleep."

"Your mom said Rebecca came by to see you and that she waited for the longest time. She asked if you could go by tomorrow."

I fluffed my pillow and sank my head into the middle just the way I liked it best. I couldn't think about Rebecca. My world had just changed and I wanted to feel the full beauty and wonder of it.

❧

In the cold light of day I was still a little light-headed. I stood at the woodstove frying up cod tongues for breakfast and my hands were making all the right motions but all I could think about was being joined in love. I daydreamed about being married. We could go to bed early, do it in the morning and even in the middle of the afternoon, especially on Sundays when there was no fishing and no housework.

"You will be hot in that woolly turtleneck. Won't be snow for a few weeks yet," said Kate as she came in from the outhouse. I couldn't tell if she was being saucy about the hickeys on my neck or what. I wasn't sure she even knew what a hickey was.

We swept and dusted, finished the basket of ironing, baked jam-jams and fixed a boat for the twins that they could float down our brook. Finally after supper the chores were caught up and we figured we would go Down Below to see what was up with Rebecca. Aunt Grace was at a Ladies' Aid meeting that would go on forever at the other end of the Cove and Uncle Wilf always went to bed early so I knew the coast would be clear. Old Robert Gordon wasn't mooning around either because we saw him working on his boat before we turned off from our lane.

Rebecca already had company. We didn't notice right away because her company was upstairs. Rebecca was putting two mugs of tea on a tray when we walked into the kitchen. She had no choice but to invite us up for the show.

It turned out that Mabel Smith was in her bedroom with her "Professional Beauty Kit" spread out on the bed. There were three different kinds of scissors for cutting hair, eyebrow tweezers, nail scissors, neck trimmers, and some stuff I had never seen in my life. There was water in Rebecca's washbowl and a chair was near the washstand. Two lamps with fresh wicks were set on the floor near the chair.

"You may as well see this," she said as she led us into her room. "I'm getting my braid cut off. You can witness my first haircut."

Mabel earned a few dollars doing hairstyling and barbering. It was tough to make a go of it in the Cove because most folks cut their own hair or had someone in the family trim it.

She got welfare for being a single mother, but it was barely enough for food.

"We are getting her ready to snare a man," Mabel said, laughing. "The girl is sixteen in a few weeks. High time she got herself a boyfriend. 'Course, that's not really a problem, is it now, Rebecca?" She gave my cousin an elbow in the side and a big saucy wink.

Mabel threw me her pack of cigarettes and I lit one for the both of us using the matches set aside to light the lamps. I was a little taken aback that Rebecca was letting us smoke in her perfect princess room and I almost fell through the floor when Little Miss Goody Two-Shoes blasted me for not giving her a cigarette.

"Come on, Melinda, don't be greedy, light one for me too." Kate's eyes were as big as saucers.

Mabel was debating whether to hack off the braid or comb it out and cut straight across. I was not enjoying this but being practical, I reminded her the scissors wouldn't go through the braid, no matter how sharp, so she'd better undo the elastics. Mabel nodded and in a flash, Rebecca's glossy, raven hair was in ripples over her shoulders and spilling over the edge of her chair. Mabel was hovering with the scissors.

"Does your mom know about this?" Kate asked.

"We didn't get a chance to talk about it, if that's what you mean. But she said the other day that my hair was getting a bit messy so I don't expect her to be surprised."

Hmmmmm. Aunt Grace didn't know a thing. Here we were getting into trouble again because as sure as there were sinners in hell, my aunt would blame me for this. So I figured that if I'm in for a penny, I might as well do real damage.

"Hack off a foot so we can see how it looks," I ordered. The scissors flashed and Rebecca could sit on a chair without having to clear her hair for the first time in years. Kate the coward said it looked great and that we should stop. But Rebecca was determined to see a difference.

"Take it up the middle of my back," she said so loud we all jumped.

We tried to work it into a beehive but there was still too much hair. Mabel suggested she cut it short in the front for the Brigitte Bardot look. We all glared at her. Our Rebecca was not a sex kitten. If she was going to keep it this length the only practical option was a braid and not much had changed.

"Cut it to my shoulders, Mabel, and do it now before I lose my nerve." It was done and the pile of hair on the floor grew to cover Mabel's ankles. Shoulder-length was okay, but I couldn't keep my mouth closed so I blurted out that it didn't do much for her heart-shaped face.

Mabel asked about the Doris Day look, cut to just under the ears with bangs. We agreed that might be perfect and this time Mabel took a lot longer as she shaped the hair in the back into a curve and kept cutting the front so the two sides were even. It came out about an inch shorter than we'd planned.

Rebecca grabbed the hand mirror and took a long look. "Good, that's done. Now for the eyebrows." It was like she was in a mad race, and I was afraid to ask what the prize was.

Kate and I sat on the bed. The party was getting a little glum. We lit the two lamps but they didn't cheer us up. Rebecca said ouch with every tweezer pull and there was a lot to be done. She wanted her black bushy brows taken down to a fine arched line. Mabel showed her how to use eyebrow pencil, eyeliner and mascara and she had pots of foundation and rouge and tubes of lipstick spread out on the washstand.

By eleven o'clock my aunt wouldn't have recognized her daughter. She looked good. My cousin was pretty anyway and I have to say Mabel learned a few tricks at the vocational training school. The short bangs made Rebecca look pert and fresh, especially with her straight hair tucked behind her ears. The eyebrows gave her a permanent surprised look, and the lipstick made her heart-shaped mouth pouty. It was a pretty package, but my cousin had disappeared.

"What do you think, my maids, I doll up real good, eh?"

Kate shook herself awake and mumbled the first thing that came into her head. "Will you wear all that gunk to school, Rebecca?" she asked.

"Now that's an interesting question," Rebecca said. "I haven't been thinking too much about school lately. What about you, Melinda? Are you going back?" Mabel was tidying up her things and was all ears.

My Matt's engagement ring was dangling on a string between my breasts. I could feel the warmth of his body just by closing my eyes. School was the furthest thing from my mind.

"Me and Mom are still going at it like cats and dogs. She's desperate for me to finish high school," I answered.

Rebecca didn't ask Kate about school. It seemed I was the only one who knew that Kate and Chas were seeing each other every evening. They'd been together most of the summer, a record for Chas. He was twenty-three, a year older than my Matt and no doubt needing a wife, not a schoolgirl.

Kate held her tongue. She knew when to keep quiet.

Mabel, on the other hand, was bursting to tell us what we should be doing.

"Girls," she said, "marriage is a must but schooling is a good thing too. Don't knock it. Especially if you got the brains like your crowd does. I've been sending off letters to offices in Toronto and they all want a high school diploma and shorthand. Good thing I went to beauty school, at least I got that to fall back on. But I don't know if I'll ever earn enough to send for Jimmy to live with me on the mainland. He's a real good little boy and my mom and dad like having him but I want to raise him myself. I know you're thinking that if I'd married Jimmy's daddy I wouldn't have this trouble now. The way I see it is that Jimmy's dad was a real good man until I got pregnant. Then he went back on the bottle and lost his job at the mill when he beat up his boss. I'm better off taking care of the two of us than married to a no-good man. Lottie can have that life but it's not for me. How's a girl supposed to know about a boy when his family and friends don't tell her about the liquor?"

That was the first time I ever heard Mabel's story. Like everyone else around here, I believed she was a slut.

"Now, none of the nice boys here want to marry damaged goods. They like to play around and tease but they're only after one thing and when they don't get it, they spread all kinds of nasty gossip. I heard last week I did it with three guys in one of the fish shacks. I know what my reputation is in the Cove. It don't bother me but I worry about what all the gossip will do to Jimmy when he goes to school. I made one mistake and I'll be paying for it the rest of my life if I stay here. I thought we were going to be married. That's why I went all the way."

I wanted to say how sorry I was to have misjudged her but of course I didn't. We are Newfoundlanders, for God's sake, and we don't apologize.

"Thank you for coming over tonight, Mabel. Here's the two dollars for the haircut and another dollar for all the help with the makeup," said Rebecca.

"Bless you, maid. The makeup was for fun but I'll put the extra dollar aside to buy Jimmy a pair of shoes. You look real good. The boys will be after you like a bitch in heat. Oh, dear, that's not a proper thing to say in Grace Derby's home. But you know what I mean. I've got to be getting home." She made her little speech while she was packing up her bag and we walked her to the door.

My cousin made us a cup of tea and brought out a whole plate of chocolate fudge. Some had nuts and some had raisins. She made the absolute best fudge.

It was almost like old times again. Trouble was, I couldn't get comfortable talking to her, fudge or no fudge. I didn't know the person sitting across from me with the page bob and the scarlet mouth. Kate reminded Rebecca that she hadn't answered the question about school.

"That's why I came to see you two last night. I wanted to see what you are doing about school, Melinda. If you don't go back to school, I might not either. My mom is real strange. It's like she's afraid of something, like she's waiting for something to happen. Her mind is off somewhere else. Dad doesn't know what's going on and he's puzzled that he can't fix things up like old times. It's got so dreary around here. I've been talking to Mabel about driving to Toronto with her. Or you and I could have a double wedding. Robert needs someone to look after him and he does have a nice house. Toronto or Robert, what do you think?"

I didn't want to touch that one with a ten-foot fishing pole. Was it only six weeks ago that we were sitting on the rocks outside our cave talking about boys, lipstick, exam results and going away to the States.

Aunt Grace's lies and secrets were causing all the trouble. If it weren't for my aunt trying to pull the wool over everyone's eyes, Rebecca and me would likely be in Boston right this minute eating cherries picked off a tree. Life was some hard sometimes.

I just laughed at Rebecca's question and told her not to be so foolish, but I was worried to my bones.

Kate kept giving me the eye to finish up. She wanted to be

out of the way when Aunt Grace came home. I had to leave half the plate of fudge and I was still licking my fingers as we headed Upalong.

While the memory of the melting sugar was still in my mouth, I made up my mind that I would go to see Aunt Grace again because I had to. We were losing Rebecca.

And I knew I hadn't answered Rebecca's question about going back to school. I couldn't think what words to let slip from my tongue. And that's the God's truth.

CHAPTER TWELVE

❧

One for sorrow

I couldn't get up enough nerve to go into Aunt Grace's house. I hid in the darkness to see what my aunt was up to and the most I saw over the next two nights was Rebecca going out arm in arm with Robert Gordon. That was enough to make me even more determined to talk to my aunt.

On the third evening I got lucky. Just after supper Aunt Grace came out her side door wearing a light sweater and scarf and carrying spades and a garden tub. I followed her to the cemetery. I watched as she got on her hands and knees and started pulling up weeds around my grandfather's grave. Memorial Sunday was a few days away, but trust my aunt to get a jump on everyone else in cleaning up the family plot.

She saw my shadow and leaned back, shading her eyes. A streak of dirt smudged her forehead.

"So it's you, Melinda. I've wanted to see you. Here, grab a spade and help me pull these dandelions up. We want our graves to be tidy when the family comes out to pay respect to our dead."

I stooped down across the grave from her. Our shadows touched and I flinched. She didn't give me a chance to open my mouth.

"I noticed something the other day and going over it in my head, I think you're the person who might know what's going on. A certain piece of paper is missing and I'm pretty sure my daughter doesn't have it. I've kept my eye on her and I think she knows something, but not everything on the document. Then it struck me how you looked at me with total disbelief a few weeks ago during our discussion. I think you might know where it is."

She stopped, leaving a big silence. I found a whole bunch of weeds that needed my devoted attention. She waited as I struggled with what to do, what to say. Then she found my eyes and locked on. My aunt never lacked nerve, I give her that.

"I want it back, I don't want any questions and I want you to forget you ever saw whatever you think you saw."

"And what about Rebecca? Do we forget about her, too? Do we just let her quit school, give up her drawing and marry a man more than twice her age who wants nothing more than his meals on the table and a wife in his bed? Is that what you want, Aunt Grace?" Her head was down again and she clawed at the weeds, pulling each straight out by the roots using her bare hands.

"It looks to me that my daughter has made up her own mind about what she wants. It makes no odds in the end. She would have married someone here and raised my grandchildren after teachers' college. Everything is just a few years ahead of schedule. Robert will provide for her," she said quietly.

"So you still don't believe that she wants to leave the Cove, go to Toronto and never come back again," I said. This was a bit harsh but I was good and angry. I had to make her see things were much worse than she imagined.

There was silence. Then I heard a whisper of a voice.

"She can't leave. She's everything to Wilf, everything," said my aunt.

It was the first time I saw Aunt Grace look unsure of herself. She fumbled for her keys and asked me to follow her into the church.

But whatever she had to say went unsaid. Just as we sat down we heard shouting coming from the lane.

"Is Mrs. Derby there?" someone was hollering. My aunt was at the door in an instant.

"Thank God we found you, Mrs. Derby," said one of the Kennedy children. "It's Lottie. The baby is coming early and she don't look too good. Lottie told me to come find you."

Aunt Grace was out the door clipping on the heels of the child.

What could I do but chase after her? She turned at the church gate, stopped and sent me to her house to get sheets, a bottle of iodine, the big sharp knife and her special tongs. Just in case, is what she said.

I was breathless when I got to the Kennedy house. The kids were all hanging around the bedroom door and the oldest one told me their mother was resting in her bedroom with a headache, which meant a hangover. The whole crowd of them was just useless. I shooed the children outside, went into the bedroom with my bundle and the first thing I noticed was Lottie lying very still. Her face was bruised and swollen. Her dark hair was a mass of wet tangles. Aunt Grace was wiping Lottie down with a cool cloth but she came over to me right away and spoke in a whisper.

"The children tell me she had a fight with Jamie last night and she fell over the back steps. She's gone into an early labor and it doesn't look good. She says there's not much pain, but she feels too weak to push. I want you to find Chas. Send him to our end of the road in his truck and find out if we can get through. If there's any chance we can make it over the road, we will want to try. Then go to the wharf and tell Charlie Mullen and his father that we may need to take Lottie into hospital on the ferry. Tell him we'll know within the hour and that we'll have to leave right away. They'll know what to do. Now run. Don't stop for any foolishness along the way."

With that little sting I was off. I climbed over the Kennedys' rotten fence, ran across the field and almost slid down the gravel pit behind Chas's store. He was behind the counter serving but took one look at me, gasping for breath at the door, and he left Mrs. Barnes's potatoes in the bin to come to me.

Even while I was talking, he was taking off his apron, finding his keys, was out the door. I took a minute to find one of the hired men to tell him Chas had to go out and the store needed minding.

Then I found Charlie Mullen and his dad. Good thing, too, that my aunt had planned things out. They had bits of the engine of the *Irene L.* lying all over the dock. Once I told them what was up they started putting it all together again. Charlie offered to come to Lottie's to give a hand as soon as the boat was ready. Then I ran all the way back up to Lottie's, taking the main drag. By this time the Kennedy children had spread the word that Lottie was going to have her baby. People were smiling at me as I ran past. No one knew then how much trouble was ahead.

I had never helped deliver a baby before but I figured I might as well learn what I could from my aunt. I had only been gone a half-hour, but things were much worse in the birthing room.

"She's getting weaker and weaker and I can't feel any movement from the baby. I hope Chas gets here soon. I'm beginning to think that the road is our only chance. Lottie should have called for me hours ago," said Aunt Grace. That stopped me cold in my tracks. I was pretty sure this was not what Lottie had in mind when she talked about having her baby in the hospital.

We waited. The house had got real quiet. Even the kiddies knew things weren't right. Lottie didn't whimper, nothing. She just lay there as if in a deep, deep sleep.

Then we heard a commotion and Jamie was hammering at the bedroom door. We both went to him. He was so drunk he latched onto the doorjamb to stay standing.

"I want my wife. You old busybodies, get out of my bedroom," he slobbered.

My aunt steered him out of the room and closed the door, leaving me with Lottie.

But I could hear what was going on. Aunt Grace was telling Jamie in a low, harsh voice that Lottie must have *fallen* pretty hard over the back steps to get those bruises on her face.

If anything happened to Lottie, she said, it could turn into a matter for the justice of the peace. I couldn't tell if Jamie was laughing or sobbing, but he pestered my aunt to believe it had been an accident, that he tried to catch Lottie when she fell. Finally he went away and Aunt Grace came back to the room looking drained. Then Chas was at the door.

"I'm sorry, Mrs. Derby. There's no chance of getting through on the road. There's a bit of that big cliff around the back of Cook's Point still to be blasted away. There's no way around it. And the road is very rough, with just the rock base for a few miles. Another week and we might get through. Not now. We'll have to take her on the ferry." Just then Charlie walked in and Aunt Grace, her shoulders just a little more stooped, prepared Lottie for the move.

Lottie was lying on a thin mattress. Beneath the bruises she was as white as death, and her breathing was so low I had to look twice to believe she was alive. Aunt Grace tucked the blankets in tight around her right up to her chin, told the boys to lift her on the mattress and put her very gently in the truck. Aunt Grace picked up her bundle and followed the home-made stretcher. She motioned me to come too.

By this time the word had spread that Aunt Grace was taking Lottie into the hospital. Folks lined up along the road looked miserable. They all knew that hospitals were where people went when Aunt Grace needed serious help. Even the Kennedy children looked decently solemn. Chas drove slowly, easing over every pothole like he was carrying Lottie in his arms.

At the wharf Charlie's dad had the engine running, a little putt-putt of hope. Chas and Charlie eased Lottie aboard. She was a rag doll blown up like a balloon. Aunt Grace got herself settled in the tiny cabin and Chas put Lottie's head on her lap and my aunt wrapped her hand around Lottie's wrist. I sat at the end of the bench and took her feet. They were cold as ice. Chas got his last instructions to send a telegram to the hospital and ask for an ambulance to be at the government wharf in two hours' time. Captain Mullen was already pulling away from the dock and Chas had to jump to get clear.

We sat in silence for the longest time. Aunt Grace moved her lips in prayer and I was willing Lottie to open her eyes and tell us she was sorry about giving us such a bad scare.

The *Irene L.* took most of a day on her normal run into the city. She stopped to pick up and deliver mail, supplies and passengers at four harbors along the way, coming and going. But tonight the engine was going flat out and Captain Mullen had her in a straight line headed in the Bay, toward Corner Brook.

An hour passed. Lottie was breathing, just barely, and I felt in my heart we were going to make it. Aunt Grace and I sat, almost touching, linked by Lottie. Then I was almost startled out of my skin when Aunt Grace shattered the silence.

"The baby is gone. There was nothing we could do. It was dead by the time we got to the Kennedys'. Lottie is pretty bad. I want you to know that. I want you to be ready for the worst. When this kind of thing happens there's nothing neither you nor I could do. Two hours is too long but I had to give her that chance. A half-hour on the road and she might have been okay."

A mere five or six minutes later, Lottie took her last shallow breath. I hardly noticed the difference but my aunt was holding her wrist and she uttered a deep sob when Lottie's heart stopped beating. I knew for certain when Aunt Grace asked me to help lay Lottie out on the floor of the cabin and tidy her up.

I cried with a pain as big as the setting sun as I braided her heavy hair, just the way she wore it until she got married. Aunt Grace slipped up top to tell Captain Mullen. He didn't cut his speed, just kept going, pushing into the crests of the waves, into the darkening night.

The ambulance men knew, just looking at our faces. The young RCMP officer who was there with the ambulance stood at attention and saluted while Lottie's body was carried ashore. His hands trembled as he took the particulars of her short life. Then he pulled himself together, motioned Aunt Grace aside, and asked about the bruising.

And didn't my aunt tell him straight out that she'd been told that Lottie had an accident, a nasty fall that was no one's fault but her own carelessness. We keep our problems to ourselves, we do. He then assured us he would take care of every-thing and that he'd let Aunt Grace know when Lottie would be ready to come back to the Cove.

⌐

With that there was nothing more for us to do but to get back on the ferry and ride home into an aching night. We settled back into the cabin, in exactly the same positions, only this time tired to the bone and numb.

Once we were well out into the middle of the Bay and fol-lowing a silver moon home, Aunt Grace started talking, so quietly that I had to lean in to her to pick up the words.

"Seeing Lottie die has made me realize how really awful it would be if Rebecca were to leave the Cove. Leaving your family for good is a little like dying. And after the way you helped me tonight, Melinda, I think you're old enough to hear the story of Rebecca's birth. But I'm warn-ing you," she said, "once you know the truth, you will have a responsibility to help me protect Rebecca, Wilf and the family."

With the lops pushing against the boat and the two of us sitting in near darkness, she began telling me the story.

"I wasn't a young woman when I joined the Red Cross. I was twenty-five, an old maid. I didn't know if Wilf would come back from the fighting. I was beside myself with worry about him and he never sent any letters. Being so isolated here, so far from the war news, was tormenting me. I begged Nan to let me go to Boston until she couldn't say no any longer. I worked all hours, played the piano for the wounded men, wrote letters and tended the boys who wouldn't be going home. Everything you've heard about the Red Cross and my work at the hospital in Boston, is true—except I always left out Harry, Henry Ellis.

"Harry was a Bostonian from the kind of family we were

before my father died. He tried to go overseas but he had broken a leg while sailing and he had a limp. Instead he came out to the hospital to volunteer. He was charming and easy with people. He always took on the hardest cases, trying to comfort the dying men. Then one Saturday morning we bumped into each other in a little coffee shop near Boston Common. After that we met most Saturday mornings and we got to know each other over apple pie, coffee and a cigarette. Yes, I used to smoke back then. He came to the hospital almost every day. He listened to me talk about how much I missed Cook's Cove and the worries I had about my family. Several of my cousins were missing in action at the time. Herb was on his way home wounded. I didn't know where Wilf was. Harry never mentioned his family but talked about the opera and books and films. It took my mind off the bad things. He didn't seem to have a job and got into the habit of showing up just when my shift was over.

"It dawned on us one Saturday as we huddled in the rain in Harvard Square that we were more than friends. I was telling Harry that I had a leave coming up and was planning to go home to Newfoundland. He said he couldn't bear not seeing me for a month.

"I didn't go home after all. It was wartime and maybe that and my worries made me reckless. The truth is that I moved into his apartment with him for my leave. I loved him very, very much and it seemed to be the right thing to do. I discovered he was a painter and I would sit for hours in his studio and watch him and even model for him. Sometimes I would tell him about the Cove and he would paint me pictures to make me feel at home. We hardly went out. He was very generous, and had flowers and chocolates and even jewelry delivered to the apartment almost every day. Sometimes his friends would come by and we'd have a bottle of wine and whatever I could cook up in his tiny kitchen. We were very happy. For a short time.

"Then as the month came to a close he changed. He brought home bottles of hard liquor that he would sit and drink by himself. I asked one of his friends what had happened and he explained to me that Harry's family had turned him out because of his drinking. The friend told me that Harry had only been sober since helping out at the hospital and finding me. But, he told me, Harry's family had just made it clear they were against him marrying a girl with no connections or money. A few days later, in a drunken rage, Harry asked me to leave and told me he never wanted to see me again.

"The pain was almost unbearable. He disappeared from my life except for the times I saw him on the Common drinking whiskey straight out of bottles he was hiding in his pocket.

"Out of the blue Wilf showed up a couple of weeks later, in January of 1943. His ship needed a refit and the crew was put ashore in the States. I was off duty and pretty hurt and lonely when he tracked me down.

"I was so comfortable with him. He had known me since I was a child, he was from the Cove, he was my cousin. He made me laugh again. I believed I could forget Harry and rekindle my old love for Wilf. We even tried to get married while he was in Boston but the paperwork was difficult since we weren't Americans. Wilf sailed away and a few weeks later I got a letter from his mother saying that he was missing in Southeast Asia. I was aching to come home but I couldn't because by then I knew I was having a baby and I wasn't married. My prayers were answered when Harry came around saying he missed me and he promised not to drink another drop of alcohol. I moved back in with him and I let him think the baby was his. I knew it was a terrible thing to do but I had to give the baby a name. It wasn't long before he started drinking again. He came to the hospital when Rebecca was born and he signed his name to the birth registry. Then he walked out of the maternity ward and disappeared. Just vanished.

"I had no money to speak of, a new baby, no husband. I was a foreigner. I stayed in Harry's apartment and sold his paintings and whatever bits and pieces I could. When Rebecca was three months old I pulled myself together and got work as a waitress. The bleak months went by and just when I wasn't sure I could hang on a moment longer, Wilf's parents sent a letter saying he'd been a prisoner of war and was in hospital in Halifax and that he would recover a lot faster if I went to him. It was all he talked about, they said, even in his troubled sleep. I packed up and went to Halifax. I was frightened but had no need to be. He was thrilled about having a child and shouted for the minister to marry us immediately.

"I don't want to hurt Wilf. You have been in my room. You know we don't live as man and wife. At first he was too ill and then, for me, well, it never felt right. Over the years Rebecca has become more important to him than anything else in the world. She can't go to the mainland. She is his anchor in a life that neither of us expected to turn out this way. He's been so generous to me. I owe him the respect of his daughter.

"He knows nothing about Harry, or about whose name is on the birth certificate and when Rebecca was born. Before we came back to the Cove I left Rebecca's papers out on my dressing table for him to accidentally see so I could explain everything to him. I felt so guilty about the time I spent with Harry. That's when I found out he couldn't read a word. He's ten years older than me and when he was a youngster, boys went fishing when they were eight and nine years old.

"Now there's something else. I always thought Harry died from his drinking. But that Mr. Harris who came by this summer was a good friend of Harry's. He told me that Harry is now a well-established artist in Boston who is known for his nude paintings. Mr. Harris told me there's a very nice one at the Museum of Fine Arts of a tall blond woman done in 1943. I'm terrified that if Rebecca goes to Boston she'll never come back to us again. She'll find a man who may well claim her as his daughter, who is charming, has money, a place in the world and who can open many doors for her. We all have so much to lose. Don't you see that, Melinda? Wilf will have to be told and it will break him. I won't have him hurt.

"Rebecca will leave all of us. People here will know about my past and they'll only see the bad, not the good. I need you to help me, Melinda. Rebecca listens to you. If you tell her I've got her best interests at heart, she'll believe you. She trusts you. Please, Melinda. I've never begged for anything in my life, but I beg of you now, help me to hold this family together."

I didn't want to know any of this. Really, this is not what I had bargained for when I said I would help my cousin back at the cave.

"I want you to promise, Melinda, with Lottie's soul as your witness, that you'll stand by the family. You've got to help me keep Rebecca here in the Cove."

My tongue was thick and stubborn. It wouldn't twist to form the words. Protecting the family meant destroying Rebecca's future as an artist. Even I could see that.

All of this was jumbling through my brain. Aunt Grace was waiting. I couldn't see a way out. An early marriage for Rebecca would keep the peace, keep the family in good standing and most of all, allow Uncle Wilf to continue doting on his precious daughter. All I had to do was convince Rebecca that staying in the Cove was the right thing to do.

I had been watching my hands twisting in my lap. In truth, I didn't know what to say. A solemn promise was beyond me and that's what I was just about to say when we heard voices coming to us from our government wharf.

It was Chas and Kate trying to calm a drunken Jamie. I bolted out of the cabin and went up on deck to see how close we were, just fifty yards off. Aunt Grace came up behind me, more slowly, more dignified, considering the bad news she had to deliver. I got out of making a promise, but I knew she would be waiting.

It was strange though what happened when I walked home. I didn't want to talk to anyone and I kept my head down. I fished in my pockets and found some stones I'd collected the time we were skipping them near our cave. Without thinking I started throwing them into bushes along the road, real hard. And wouldn't you know it, out of one bush flew a momma crow and her six young ones. *Seven for a secret*. Enough to keep my mouth shut about what Aunt Grace told me for a long, long time.

⌖

Three days later we stood in the churchyard and said our final goodbyes to Lottie. The doctors had taken the baby from her womb but Aunt Grace thought it best just to lay the little boy in the casket with Lottie, tucked into her arms. He was perfectly formed and the two of them looked like they were down for an afternoon nap. The death certificate said she died from internal bleeding. The foreman of the road gang turned out in a black suit to pay his respects. He'd decided the whole tragedy was his responsibility because the road was behind schedule. He worked his men all weekend to open enough road for the minister to get through. Jamie stayed drunk for the wake and the burying and was already winking at us girls when they laid Lottie in her grave. The murdering bastard.

❧

Two for joy

The days washed away with the tides. We weeded the potato patch, kept the twins clean, swept, washed, baked and picked up mail. We cruised the main drag at night and went to the movie in the school hall on Saturday nights. Charlie Mullen hooked up his generator to a second-hand projector and if it didn't break down we saw the latest Roy Rogers or Abbott and Costello. About once a month Charlie brought in something more risky like *The Pajama Game* with Doris Day or Elvis in *Love Me Tender*. Kate reminded us they had Technicolor on big screens in the city.

The trip to Boston went out with the tide after the middle of August and never came back. The art course would have started and that was the end of it.

Word got around that Rebecca was smoking behind her mother's back. She was hardly at home anymore and if I went looking for her there, she wouldn't be in the kitchen. Instead she'd be in her room painting her nails and plucking her eyebrows or reading about teenage moms giving birth to babies with no brains. She chewed wad after wad of pink gum and blew gross bubbles. Her room, with its big brass bed, tiny blue rosebud wallpaper and hooked rugs, was a mess. Every piece of clothing she'd worn in the past week was on the floor, exactly where she'd taken it off. Even her dirty underwear, something we didn't talk about and certainly didn't leave out for people to see. She kept the lace curtains closed and the blinds down, so there was a good chance of tripping over something. The old familiar scent of sun-and-sea-dried linen was replaced by the smell of unwashed underarms and cheap perfume. She stopped making up the bed. It used to be the first thing she did every morning, almost before her foot touched the floor.

I only ever saw her take up a pencil once the rest of the summer.

When I couldn't find her in her bedroom I would automatically walk down to her dad's wharf but she was never there, either. Her dad would be slaving away, doing double the work, and with no one to get his mug-ups ready. I'd get him his tea and hardtack, ask if he'd seen her and he'd always say he was expecting her any minute. I'd wait a bit and she'd never show up. When I got desperate and had to convince myself that she was still in the Cove, that she hadn't run away, I'd walk up past the post office to Mabel's or down the other end of the Cove to Robert's.

When she was at Mabel's I'd have to get by Mr. and Mrs. Smith who were still so depressed about Lenora dying in the spring that every visit was like attending a wake. Lenora was Mabel's younger sister and she died of the TB. I'd look at all of Lenora's photos, right from the one in her coffin in her white confirmation dress to the baby pictures. Only after a cup of tea and a few coconut squares could I ask if Mabel was in and her mom would wave me along the hall to Mabel's room. Usually that's where Mabel, Rebecca and little Jimmy were. Hiding out. Rebecca would be teaching Jimmy how to blow bubbles with her pink gum or teaching him how to do his letters, while Mabel went through fashion magazines looking for new hairstyles and makeup. Or Rebecca would be helping Mabel write to addresses in Toronto asking about jobs. Mabel's spelling and handwriting were none too good so mostly Rebecca wrote the letters. Sometimes they'd just be talking about boys, the ones they had crushes on and the ones who gave them the eye when they passed them on the road.

When Rebecca was at Robert's I hated to go in. I'd only visit in the morning when I knew he'd still be fishing. She'd be there doing all the things she used to do for her mother. Baking the bread, doing the washing, doing up a batch of cookies or squares for mug-ups, washing the kitchen floor, ironing Robert's shirts, making his home brew. Somehow she'd come to taking care of his house for him without even an engagement ring on her finger. We all knew she slept at home every night. Aunt Grace wouldn't have allowed anything else. Still and all it was like they were practically living together and that was about as sinful as a girl could get around here. I had never ironed one of my Matt's shirts and wouldn't dream of it until after we were married.

She wouldn't listen to me. Even Mabel told me that if Rebecca wanted to come to Toronto with her, she'd have to smarten up. Mabel said she didn't want Rebecca to ruin her reputation.

I developed an upset stomach that never went away. At first I thought it was nerves. I felt sick every time I ran into Aunt Grace. I avoided her at every turn and probably vexed her to no end. I didn't want to promise her anything and avoiding the person who ran the Cove was no easy task. While I believed what Aunt Grace had told me after Lottie died, the more I thought about it, the more I thought something was missing. I couldn't put my finger on it though and that vexed *me* to no end.

My upset stomach never cleared and the third week in August I missed my monthly. I didn't need a doctor to tell me what was wrong and I dreaded having to tell my mom.

In the summertime the mail came twice a week. The *Irene L.* tied up at the government wharf around three and one of the men from Chas's store drove the filthy white canvas bags up to Nellie Lewis's place in Bottom Creek. The post office was at the Creek because that's the mid-point around the harbor and it gave all four outports about the same hour's walk. Everyone loved to go and get the mail, but most of the time it was the children who did the walking. It took Nellie an hour and a half to sort the mail and then we were barking at her door to get letters from cousins in the city and in the States and Toronto, the bill from Eaton's, or a newspaper or a circular sent by the government or the fishermen's union. The best days were when the Eaton's catalogues came in. We practically ran to the post office when we saw the bulky brown packages going up in the truck. Another good day was when the baby bonus came. It was six dollars for the younger children and eight dollars for children between ten and sixteen. My mom started giving me my share when I turned fifteen. I was saving it for my wedding dress. She thought I spent it all on foolishness. Not a penny. It was in a jar under my bed.

The most important day for students in high school was when the exam results came in. Every year about a dozen youngsters in the Cove, spread over grades nine, ten and eleven, wrote the public exams. They were marked in St. John's and the results were mailed out toward the end of August.

Word got around real fast the day the marks were in the

mailbag. Kate offered to keep me company for the walk to the post office. Luckily, we met Rebecca coming from Mabel's just as we got to Nellie's gate.

The post office was in Nellie's old summer kitchen. It was a temporary lean-to built onto the main house a good fifty years ago. The pattern on the floor canvas was worn off but clean. The counter was high and wide and you had to be careful of the aluminium edges where they'd come up a little. Or the nails, where they'd popped. Nellie had an old-fashioned pot-bellied stove off to the side and she kept it at a roar on winter days but the warmth merely kissed the room and then went looking for mischief out through the thin walls.

There was a line at the wicket when we three arrived. Nellie liked to have a yarn with each customer. She'd never ask what was in the letter or parcel, but you were beholden to let her know in a general way what was inside. We took our place.

"A coat from the fall sale catalogue, I hope this one fits. You know, Nellie, the last one was too tight across my hips."

"Bless my Aunt Gertie for sending this scented powder from Toronto for my birthday. Yardley is my favorite."

"We finally got me dad's refund from Eaton's. It was silly of him to buy records when we don't have a hi-fi."

"A letter from my brother out in Alberta. He still remembers the Cove all right."

"My grandad is sickly and the veterans' home wants my mom to go see him. Not likely that my mom can get to St. John's."

We waited through all the happiness and heartbreak. Nellie had no closing time. She stayed at the wicket until all the mail was gone.

She gave us a big grin when it was our turn. The winter catalogues first, one for me and one for Rebecca and a discussion on the new coats on the cover. Then with a queenly swish of a hand she produced official-looking letters for me and Rebecca. And a telegram for Kate from her mom and dad.

"Youse are the first ones to come for the marks," Nellie told us as she handed them over, into our shaking hands.

The emblem of the Government of Newfoundland, Department of Education, was stamped on the back. Lions and unicorns standing upright and on guard. Nellie was waiting.

"My mom is dying to order some new lace for the altar and she's desperate for the catalogue," said Rebecca.

"Well, if Grace Derby is waiting, you had better run along then. I'm sure you girls did real good on your exams." The disappointment was written across Nellie's face.

We walked a little down the road, anxious to find a place to open the envelopes without having the whole Cove stick their noses in our business. We headed for the path that took us down over the cliffs and along the beach.

We tossed coins and Rebecca had to open hers first. Pretty good. A quick bit of math showed about an 85 percent average, all the grades in a neat cluster. Kate ripped open her telegram and after the congratulations from her parents, we saw that she too had managed about an 85 average with an amazing 92 in English Literature and a 91 in History. The maths, not her strong suit, were in the low 70s.

My fingers trembled. We loved each other dearly but I had always beat my cousins and they let me be the big mouth I was because I was the smart one and had the marks to prove it.

"Dear Lord," I silently prayed, "don't let me shame myself now. This is my last chance to show I'm the one dealt the real brains in the family. I may not be the eldest anymore, but let me be the smartest."

Rebecca was over my shoulder and snatched the results out of my hands.

"This is absolutely amazing, Melinda," she screamed. "What do you think, Kate, about a 94 average. These are the best marks I've ever heard of for the provincial exams. You'll do grade eleven with bells on your toes!"

I ignored the pain of that last remark. Instead I screeched out across the harbor with her—*Eat fish, get brains!* We splashed into the icy water and danced a heady jig around the boulders.

The news zoomed around the Cove. It would have taken even less time if we'd opened the results in front of Nellie.

I went to the fish plant and told Mom while she was deboning a salmon. She almost split her hand open with the shock and thought the news so good she stopped work for a cup of tea. I got sent over to Chas's to buy a package of biscuits and there was a mug-up all around for my mom's mates.

As I was leaving she gave me a big hug in front of everyone and whispered that I would make the best nurse in all of Newfoundland.

That put me in a spin and reminded me that I had some hard news for her.

The next mail boat came in on Friday and Captain Mullen told a few kids hanging around the wharf that the city newspaper, the *Western Bay*, just ran a piece saying that the three top students in the grade ten provincial exams were all from the west coast. A girl from St. Bernard's Academy, Jane Peddle, came first and in second place was none other than me. Of course the kiddies ran up the road and along our lane shouting the news and waving the paper. It took my breath away. My name right there in the newspaper: Melinda Garreaux of Cook's Cove. Later I made the mail run and there was a big official envelope addressed to me. Nellie deserved this one so once I'd skimmed it I let her in on government secrets. It was a letter of congratulations from Premier Joey Smallwood himself, a voucher for a hundred dollars' worth of books and a list of scholarships to Memorial University that I would be eligible for if I finished grade eleven with "similar results."

It was a week of ups and downs. My mom couldn't stop smiling and it made her look real pretty. Even Nan was bragging. I gave them the couple of days of pride and happiness.

Just when I got up the nerve to tell my Matt my news he sent a note saying he'd been offered a few hours' work every evening on the road. There was a big push on to finish grading the road in time for the opening celebration. The note said he'd see me on Sunday.

I had to tell my mother. She was bound to notice that I spent more time in the outhouse than at the table. A baby was something that didn't go away.

I built my nerve by taking consolation in the old Eaton's summer catalogue. On page 53 there was a two-piece bridal gown in nylon and acetate lace and nylon net over rayon taffeta. The dress bodice was embroidered with sequins and simulated pearls. The skirt was in three tiers and each tier was covered in net. There was a sewn-in taffeta slip. The bolero jacket was covered in simulated pearls too and had a sequin trim. It was $37.50. Looked as good as Princess Margaret's dress to me.

Flipping a few pages I found a bridal halo in iridescent sequins. It was attached to a floor-length veil and fitted on with a plastic clip covered with more simulated pearls. That went for $3.95. On the same page there was a picture of a wedding bouquet—artificial lily of the valley and twelve icebox red roses, all put together with ribbon, bows and streamers. That was $5.95. Our Queen Mary roses were prettier but they were already finished for the summer and you couldn't count on the Paul Scarletts having a second blooming in September. Or I could have gone with a shoulder-length veil. The halo and nylon tulle veil were the same price as the floor-length net, $3.95. Shoes! I'd need white shoes, low ones because my Matt and me were the same height. There was an "illusion" heel for $4.99. Nice pointy toes.

Then my mood crashed. Page 82: "Even the healthiest pregnant figure will feel more comfortable in a full-length, elastic maternity girdle." I felt my hard and nauseous stomach and I couldn't believe that I'd be expected to push myself into a girdle.

I reached for old copies of the *Western Bay* from under my bed. I scanned the wedding announcements. "The guests registered at the Westport Inn." We didn't have to worry about that. "An all-white wedding, double-ring ceremony, the bride wore Wedgwood white, three-quarter length tulip sleeves, small chapel train, fingertip veil with rose and pearl appliqué." Sounded real pretty, and expensive. Another one. "The bride wore a full-length satin gown appliquéd with Alencon lace, having long sleeves and a portrait neck line. Her shoulder-length tulle illusion veil was held by a pearl tiara and she carried a white missal with a bouquet of white carnations and red sweetheart roses. The bridesmaids wore blue and pink nylon dresses with matching accessories and each carried a bouquet of pink carnations."

Bridesmaids! They'd be Kate and Rebecca, of course. Couldn't imagine Kate buying a new blue or pink nylon dress. Maybe the one I altered for the time might do. Seven weeks ago.

I couldn't bear much more. "The bride, given in marriage by her father, wore a semi-formal gown of net appliquéd with sequins over satin with pin-point sleeves. Her fingertip veil was held in place by a tiny close-fitting cap. She carried a bouquet of roses."

That got me thinking about my daddy and how he wouldn't see his first grandchild. And how he would have got me through this. He'd be so happy for me and not ask any questions or show any disappointment. He'd have just gone out and got a new suit so he could dance at my wedding.

I had a little cry. Next thing I knew my mom was shaking me awake and pointing to my nightdress and her watch that said almost eleven o'clock. She pulled the covers back and there was the catalogue open on the wedding dresses and the newspapers with the social notes and photos of smiling couples.

"What's this all about?" she asked with her eyes. I glanced across at Kate's bed. She was not home, a bit early for the lovebirds. It was now or never.

"Mom, I have to get married." I spoke the words but I couldn't look at her.

The silence wrenched my gut. I found her face and saw that she'd closed her eyes and was biting hard on her lower lip.

"Oh, Mom,' I said. "We only ever did it the once. I didn't think girls could get pregnant the first time. I figure I'm three weeks along. I wanted to as much as my Matt. I haven't told him yet but I think he'll be happy about the baby. I know I've disappointed you but I think it was pretty clear that I was going to marry my Matt sooner or later."

"My baby, my baby," was all she choked out as she slid onto the bed to cuddle me. Her silent tears slid down my cheeks. "It's always the same in this place. A girl doesn't stand a chance. At least your Matt is a good young man who loves you very much and he won't hurt you."

"What are you going on about?" I asked.

She held me closer still. I felt the hesitation in her body and then heard her sigh.

"The Derbys have always been a good-looking crowd. The men were tall and dark and rugged like your Uncle Wilf and the women were tall and buxom with thick, glossy hair and blue eyes.

"Then there was me. I'm smaller and I don't have the blue eyes but most folks will tell you that I was pretty enough. Your father was the best kind when he came courting. He'd sing and play the fiddle just for me and come around to help me with chores. He was gentle and kind. I've told you all these good things about your father many, many times.

"Your daddy was the most charming man ever born in this Cove. He could have given that Ricky Nelson of yours a few lessons. He sang love songs at all the parties and times. He danced so smooth you didn't know when the music stopped. He'd make sure the old ladies had a chair and a little something to drink. He loved being around women. It was nothing to find him in someone's kitchen making up a batch of tea biscuits or changing a nappy so the missus could rest her feet. Some said it was the French blood, that the Frenchies like to please their women. Like every girl in the Cove I had a crush on him from the time I was twelve. Roe went off to war in 1939, one of the first to join up and all the Cove women cried into their aprons when the boat took him away.

"He came home in 1944 after his destroyer was torpedoed out from under him. He was in the North Atlantic for hours and the medics on the Red Cross ship pronounced him dead. But I guess they didn't reckon on him being a Newfie. He pulled through all right and was sent home on medical leave. I was seventeen and because all the young men went off to fight, I'd never had a fella. They didn't see many girls in the navy either so six weeks after he set foot on the wharf we were married and I was a month gone. It all happened that fast. I wore a pink suit Nan made from a satin dress she had when she was first married. Oh, Melinda, darling, I was so happy. The man I'd always loved would be waking up by my side every day for the rest of our lives."

I could see them, you know. The wedding picture was downstairs on the old mahogany sideboard. She was skinnier than even now and the smile was as big as her face. Her bouquet was a huge trailing bunch of Paul Scarlett roses in full bloom and they were crushed between the two of them for the pose.

Then she skewered my heart.

"What I didn't know and no one told me was that your father was a hard drinker. The liquor gave him a bad temper. Over the years I figured out that no one told me because all the men here drank a lot so he wasn't any different. I don't know what the other women put up with but whenever your father had a few drinks, he hit. I took all the blows. Honey, he was a good man but maybe the war, maybe coming back here after he'd seen the world, maybe the constant headaches, changed him. Have you never wondered why there's ten years between you and the twins?

"After we married I don't think he ever came home sober. Your Uncle Wilf took him on as crew and Wilf gave me half of your father's pay to make sure we had food and winter coats. There were lots of days when I couldn't go outdoors because I was too proud to let the folks see the bruises and the nasty cuts. He was a big man and I've never been more than a hundred and ten pounds. Grace figured it all out as soon as she got home and she and Nan would cover for me. They talked to him but he wouldn't listen.

"Then a small miracle. A Salvation Army officer came to the Cove and Roe got religion. He had great respect for the Army because officers were always on the docks helping the boys during the war. He stopped drinking, cold turkey. We'd been married ten years and it took me a while to believe this was going to last. After about three months, I let him back into my bed and I got sick with the twins. Then the officer left and your dad went back on the bottle. I was seven months gone when they found his body tangled in his herring net. I couldn't even cry. I knew that he wouldn't beat me any more and the babies I was carrying would stand a chance of being born alive. We all protected you, Melinda, darling. Grace, Nan, even Wilf would come and take you away in the middle of the night if there was a racket. I warned Roe that if he ever hurt you I would cut out his eyes with a fish knife."

I slumped against my mom and absorbed the warmth of her body. I had a haunting memory of other hands putting me to bed. I'd had the feeling before and always thought it was the leftovers of a childhood dream. I remembered spending so many evenings Down Below when my mom had a headache.

This was almost more than I could bear. I couldn't believe I had never seen my father's dark side.

By the time she left my room, my mom had promised me a nice wedding. I lay awake for another hour listening to her sob herself to sleep. I refused to feel sorry for her or for me. What was done was done and I had to look ahead and make plans. First thing I had to do was tell my Matt we were having a September wedding.

I sent him a note and he eased himself into a kitchen chair the next afternoon between the fishing and the roadwork. He looked bone weary and drank a glass of home brew like it was water. I felt bad about having to add to his load.

It was foggy and damp. A week left in August and the rain was almost sleet. My Matt and me linked arms and headed to our house and we found a dry spot in the inside corner of our bedroom. The roof was on but the windows still had to be ordered and paid for.

Telling my mom was like going downstream in a canoe compared to this. My Matt waited, he didn't hurry me.

"Remember that night when we, well, when we…well, you know."

"Melinda, my love, that was a mistake. A wonderful mistake, but it is not to happen again until the minister gives us his blessing. I hope you didn't lure me here to tempt me. I came because your note sounded serious. Is it something to do with your cousins?"

I kept my head down. "There is something I have to say. I can't think of any way of saying it except straight out. Matt, darling, you're going to be a father, and well, I'm going to be a mother." That part was pretty dumb but I wasn't thinking straight.

He grabbed my hands and forced me to look him straight in the eye.

"Tell me this isn't one of your pranks." I could barely squeeze out that I was telling the truth because he had unbuttoned both our coats and was holding me so close I could smell the sea and the earth on his skin.

"How are you feeling? We've got to tell your mother. She won't like it but this changes everything and we'll get married this fall. Holy hell, I've got a whack of work to do on this house. Are you all right? You do want to get married, don't you? Our son will be some smart with you as his mom. Take the ring from around your neck so I can put it on your finger."

I was no longer a girl in trouble. I was a woman planning her wedding.

He held me so tight the entire walk home that he was a hazard to my safety. But I couldn't tell the fool anything. He was grinning and talking aloud about his plans to finish the house in a hurry, get at least the kitchen and maybe a bedroom ready before the fall fishery began in three weeks' time. Of course the outside would be tarpaper until the spring but there'd be heat and running water and maybe electric lights by November.

My mom was waiting by the woodstove, knitting a tiny sweater in the rocking chair. My Matt put on the charm.

"Mrs. Garreaux, me and Melinda got something to tell you. We want to get married this fall. I know you want us to wait but I'm afraid we got ahead of ourselves and Melinda is going to have our baby. We figures the best thing for everyone is to have a wedding as soon as we can get it all planned out. I can have the house ready by the middle of September. I'm sorry, ma'am, that this happened but Melinda and me, well, we are very happy and we ask for your blessing. I'll be getting my own fishing boat in the spring and the house is paid up so we'll be all right."

I didn't know he could take charge like that or that he had such a long speech in his head.

My mom said she could see it coming and that my Matt was a good boy. The disappointment was in the way she huddled in the chair, but she didn't speak of it.

"Melinda and me and her nan will plan the wedding and we'll make it a real good one, son."

I kissed him goodbye on the back porch and he went off down the lane whistling one of the new songs on the hit parade, "Save the Last Dance for Me." I loved that boy to pieces.

CHAPTER FOURTEEN

❧

Three for a wedding, four for a boy

August was cold, wet and blowy. But two days after I talked to my Matt, the angels sent us a day so golden, so balmy, so still that I went in search of my cousins. It had to be the cave. It was the only place I could bare my soul.

I packed a picnic basket and tucked some magazines down the side. As soon as Kate opened her eyes I told her I wanted to be on the water in the hour. I reckoned she had sneaked in the night before around two. She groaned but when she rolled over the sun splashed her face. She opened one eye and said she would be ready. I slipped out the door and walked quickly down the lane to round up Rebecca.

Aunt Grace wasn't home, thank goodness, so I went up the stairs to Rebecca's room and found her there painting her toenails and smelling of beer and cigarettes.

"After your toenails are perfect, can you come across the harbor with me and Kate?" I asked. Her arched eyebrows arched higher to ask what was up while she dripped red nail polish onto her quilt.

"Kate goes back in two weeks and with the fall weather starting early, this may be our last day of sunshine. And it's my birthday, though everyone seems to have forgotten about me this year."

She hesitated and then said, ever so slowly, "Happy birthday. Yes, I'd like that. We've got chocolate dream squares and leftover chicken."

"Can you be ready by eleven?"

"Sure. Do you want me to ask Dad for the rowboat?" It was settled like she was the old Rebecca.

Kate did the rowing. She claimed she didn't trust us in a boat. Bit cheeky. We gently tucked into the rocks and splashed into the bitter cold water. The Arctic ice had floated through the Strait of Belle Isle and down the Gulf of St. Lawrence earlier than usual. We skipped across the meadow like youngsters on the last day of school. There were still splashes of color, wild Virginia roses, foxglove and a sprinkle of fireweed, the last blaze of summer. Within ten minutes of tying up the boat, we reached our rocky perch and the cave.

"We'll cozy down here out of the wind, so you two can have a good smoke. Don't say I never think of you," said Kate. No one had noticed that I hadn't had a cigarette for the past two weeks. The smoke made me sick.

I told them I was trying to give up that foolishness.

"Must be why you're putting on a bit of weight, my maid. It looks good on you," said Rebecca. There was my opening, handed to me on a silver platter. But it was too soon. I couldn't. I was screaming inside my head but I smiled.

"I always add a few pounds in the summer," I said and changed the subject to television. There was a lot of talk about television because we were getting electricity before the winter and some folks were getting a television set before a stove or a washing machine. I grilled Kate on how a moving picture could end up in a little box. She went on in some detail about airwaves, broadcasting and antennas. I didn't understand a word, but I got a chance to stare out to sea and the waves calmed me.

Kate told us about *The Rifleman* and *I Love Lucy*. Just when I was getting excited about TV, she switched to TB. She and Chas had been listening to the *Doyle Bulletin* on Saturday night and there was a special hello to everyone in Cook's Cove from Annie Park who was in the West Coast Sanatorium with the lung disease. Kate said she promised herself she would visit Annie every weekend when she went back to school.

There we were, back to a subject I didn't want to talk about. I quickly brought out the magazines.

Rebecca got the *Teen Confessions* and Kate and I each got a *Chatelaine*. Max Factor had a new line of lipstick shades— Hi-Society in Clear Red, Dazzling Coral, Electric Pink and Pink Capri. I flipped past the rather serious-looking article on René Lévesque but marked it for Kate to read later and stopped at the photos of Brigitte Bardot marrying Jacques Charrier dressed in gingham. I flipped some more and scanned a story on the legal marrying age for Canadian girls. The age in Newfoundland was twelve. I was past my prime.

I finally found what I was looking for, the teen advice column.

I read out loud. *"I'm a bore. I don't know how to be gay and funny. I'm afraid boys will never like me.* Signed Anne in Edmonton. *Not to worry, boys like girls who will appreciate their funny remarks. A man likes to marry a woman who is warm and companionable, not necessarily sharp and witty.*

"Lord dyin'," I said. "Do you think there is a school we can go to that takes out our brains and teaches us to be warm and companionable?"

There was another one. *"My friend spent the whole evening*

flirting with my date. If my date goes out with her, I'll die. From Sally in Sudbury. It says here, *Never admit to your date that you feel wild, it will only make him find someone less moody. Tell him you are sorry about the bad arrangement and don't mention it again.* Is that what you would do if I flirted with your Charles? After you scratched out my eyes, of course."

"He's not mine and besides, you're not his type."

"Oh, dearie me. The claws are out. Now that we are on the subject, where were you last night, or should I say this morning?" Kate's eyes went narrow, like they always did when she was angry. "Be mad if you like, but a girl who is out with a boy until two in the morning is usually doing one thing."

She got real mad. "Chas had to drop in home to pick up a book he wanted me to read and his mom and dad invited me in for a cup of tea. We were all nervous but once the talk turned to books we went on for hours. His mother gets all the latest novels from a book club and his father has hundreds of books on Newfoundland politics. It was the first time I was in their house. Then Chas and I went for a long walk, past the post office, all the way over to Halfway Point."

"And that's what you expect me to believe. That you were out until two in the morning with a boy, and you had tea with his mom and dad and then you walked."

"It's the truth and I don't want to hear what you're thinking with your dirty mind." All this time Rebecca stared at us like we had truly gone around the bend. "Am I hearing things? What's going on here? Kate and Chas? I thought that was over weeks ago. Chas never lasts more than a month with a girl."

I told her that just about everyone else had missed it too so not to worry. I doubted if I would have noticed anything if Kate hadn't been sleeping three feet away from me. My

Matt said Chas never said a word to him either. As deep as the ocean, both of them.

Silence from Kate. I had her over a fish barrel. She turned her head toward me and I got in there with a sharp hook.

"I saw the way you held his arm after the movie on Saturday. You looked closer than debating buddies. When you went walking last night were you two talking about what happens after the summer?"

Kate's face struggled with my question. "Last night Chas asked me to wear his initial ring. I don't know much about how all this romance stuff works but I think wearing a boy's ring is a big step so I told him I needed to think about it."

By this time she was looking pitiful. I tossed my magazines down and took a good long look at my cousin.

I gave her a few pointers. "Wearing his ring means you're going steady and can't date other boys. It is also the ring you wear before you get an engagement ring and you know what comes after the engagement ring. So I'd say Chas asking you to wear his ring is pretty serious stuff especially considering he's twenty-three and most fellas his age are looking for wives, not dancing or debating partners. And to my knowledge, he's not asked any girl before to wear his ring."

"I'm scared."

"What are you going to do?"

"That's the problem. I'm not sure. I want to do grade eleven and go to university. If I go steady my mom will want me to start a hope chest and she'll be asking if I want to marry in the Cove or in the city. I couldn't bear it. But when I'm with Chas that's all I want. I want to help him run the business, I want to order books we can read together, I want to be with him all the time."

"It sounds like you got it bad. Come here," I said. "I can't have a heart-to-heart with you while you're shivering."

We all snuggled closer and it was easier to share secrets.

Rebecca finally figured it all out and she was busting with advice.

"You're not from here, Kate. You'll never fit in. Chas is wonderful but let me tell you what your life will be like in the Cove when the summer is over and the long winter sets in. If you marry him, folks will count on their fingers the days to when the first baby is born. If you don't have a baby right way, there'll be talk that you had a secret miscarriage, the time you went home early from the supper because you weren't feeling well. And if you don't have a baby for a couple of years folks won't be bashful about asking you if there is anything wrong with you. You'll want to believe it's no one's business, but you see, my dear, around here, everything is everyone's business. It's not for a city girl who likes to keep her cards close to her chest."

Then it was my turn.

"You won't have time to read anymore. Your days will be swallowed whole. Chas will want to know what's for supper and he won't be ready for a discussion on Churchill Falls and the government's policy on electrical power. The babies will come year after year. You'll cut your hair and get a Toni perm. You'll learn to make sweaters or doilies or cushions for the sale-of-work. You'll go to our church every Sunday and you'll be above reproach like a Derby is expected to be, especially one married into the richest family for miles around.

"Lord dyin', Kate, you're the baby of the crowd, you're smart and you've got a good tongue in your head. You're our hope that something good will happen. Your dad got away, don't you come back."

Kate could always give as good as she got but this time she took me by surprise. "Why don't you take your own advice and leave Cook's Cove? Your mom wouldn't stop you," she asked.

Rebecca was waiting for the answer, too.

I could have told them, then, about the baby, but that would not have been the truth and my cousins deserved the truth. I was thinking through my answer when Rebecca took a long draw on her cigarette, and when she spoke she laid bare my soul.

"She can't leave. I've taken a good measure of our Melinda these last couple of years. When we say goodbye to you in September I've never once heard her say she'd like to be on that ferry too. Did you see when she got that letter about the scholarship? Oh, she was happy to get her name in the paper, but when that letter said she could go to St. John's, I saw terror in her eyes. She's rooted to the Cove. She knows every laneway, every rock, every old geezer and every new baby. I honestly think that if she went among strangers, she would waste away. She can't leave. Isn't that right, Melinda?"

I didn't know it about myself but once it was out of her mouth, I knew she had captured my nature as easily as she sketched my face.

"I would have gone to Boston with you, Rebecca. And I was even thinking about looking into nursing school if we had gone. I think I could have stayed away long enough to do nursing training because I'd have known I was coming back forever."

"Yes, maid. I believe you," said Kate. And then she told us that in her own way, she had come to terms with Chas. "I guess I don't have to make a decision until the winter. Chas is buying a car in September and will drive into the city every Sunday until the snow comes."

"Wow," said Rebecca. "You two really are a couple. Robert wants to take me into Corner Brook when the road is finished to look at rings in Alteen's."

That's exactly how she told us. No softening us up, no

preparation. Kate and I instantly went on the alert.

"What kind of ring?" I asked.

That's when it all spilled out. "I've been doing a lot of thinking. My mom doesn't want me to leave the Cove. And she doesn't want anyone to know about when I was born. She's angry with me for finding out. I know I was born before she and Dad got married and she's afraid I'll tell. She's afraid that maybe folks will find out she's made mistakes like everyone else. And that she lied. I think she's genuinely sad that I might pack up the car and go with Mabel down the road to Toronto. I can sense her pushing me toward Robert because she wants to keep me here. Sometimes I think that would be easiest. Get the ring, get married, everyone happy."

She tried to tell us that Robert was the best thing that ever happened to her but when we let the silences grow, she admitted he was set in his ways and hadn't read a book or even a magazine in his entire life. He told her she would not have to worry about teachers' college because he would take care of her.

She was one confused girl. She could see Robert wouldn't be the kind of husband she dreamed about, she said, but he would do. Or maybe she'd go back to school or just go to Toronto. No matter to her where she ended up.

All of this was said in the same voice she used to tell us what color cap she was thinking of making. I wanted to scream at her to do the right thing for herself, not for Robert, not for her mother. I could see that Robert was not good for her, but no girl hears those words. I was in no position to advise her to go back to school either.

"We're still best cousins, Rebecca. Don't run off and do something without telling us about it," I said, and Kate agreed.

Rebecca reached for the gold ring she kept tied around her neck, but of course it wasn't there. She'd given the ring back to Nan and on Memorial Sunday, three weeks ago, Nan buried it at the foot of Granddad's grave and put down a square stone marker she'd had made in the city for her boy Edward.

The time had come to tell my cousins my plans for the fall. I didn't know how to begin until Kate remarked carelessly, "Melinda, my maid, here's another sandwich. You're eating like it's for two. Hope you won't be throwing up on the way home like you did all morning."

The sound of her voice mixed with the splashing waves. A seagull dived into the sea for its lunch. Both Rebecca and Kate digested the words at the same time and turned to look at me.

"Please say it's not what I'm thinking," blurted out Kate.

"Well, it is, and don't be sorry for me. Me and my Matt always planned to be married so it makes no odds. He'll be a wonderful daddy. My mom wants me to have a nice wedding and I want you two to be my bridesmaids."

They kept looking at me with their tongues hanging out so I talked nonstop like I did when I was nervous, about how happy I was and that next summer Kate was to come to stay with me, that I'd have the guest room all decked out by then with wallpaper and linoleum. Kate asked if someone getting the baby bonus could get the baby bonus for a baby. That broke us up and we all had a bellyaching laugh.

My silly cousins wouldn't let me row back. Just as well. I spent the entire half-hour heaving my guts over the side of the boat.

And of course there was a surprise cake with sixteen candles waiting for me. And presents. Blue gingham to make curtains for my new home from my mom, a hooked rug from Nan, an electric iron from my Matt and lipsticks from my cousins.

CHAPTER FIFTEEN

❧

Five for silver

We decided on September tenth—the same day the road was opening, Rebecca's birthday and three weeks after I turned sixteen. It suited everyone. My Matt said he needed at least three weeks to get the house fit to live in. September tenth gave him exactly three weeks. He quit the road job and he and his dad worked on the house until dark every night, even in the bitter wind and rain. Mom thought I might start showing since I couldn't stop eating and she thought it was best all round to have the wedding sooner rather than later.

It turned out that this was the last possible day that Kate could stay. She would miss a couple of days of registration and book-buying but real classes for her final year of high school started the following Monday. At first we didn't think it would work at all because she would have to wait another week for the ferry that went on its fall schedule in September. Then it struck us that she could simply catch a ride back with someone in a car. When Uncle Herb and Aunt Mary were told about the wedding they offered to drive out to pick up

Kate. It turned out that lots of people were coming for the big celebration of the new road, including the Anglican minister who had been invited to bless the road to the future. He agreed to stay later to marry us in the afternoon. We told everyone who came by to congratulate us to come to the wedding supper up at the school and lined up extra plates for those who would come, invited or not. We planned for more than a couple of hundred people, not counting the children.

I didn't get the wedding outfit in the catalogue after all. Nan ordered a white satin and rayon mix instead and Chas's dad used his telephone to arrange for the material to be at the wharf in the city for the next mail boat. Nan ran up a beautiful gown with a couple of hidden inverted pleats so it appeared to fit snug at the waistline and draped away to a long full skirt. She stayed up a couple of nights sewing on white sequins and tiny plastic pearls. It was perfect, better than anything you could buy at Eaton's and a third the price. I borrowed a lacy veil and white shoes from Kate's sister Susie and Mom gave me her silver locket to wear and to keep. I used my wedding dress money—the baby bonus money I'd been saving in a jar under my bed—for yellow paint for our kitchen and a down payment on a beautiful oil and electric cooking range. My mom gave her money for the upstairs oil heater to buy the fabric, the turkeys, hams, potatoes, flour, sugar, raisins and candied cherries. The wedding cake wasn't soaked in rum and aged, but it was the traditional fruit cake.

My Aunt Grace came around, just a little. We both knew I was still avoiding making her the promise she wanted. She let it go and sewed Rebecca and Kate's dresses. Rebecca jumped every time her mother's hand chanced on her skin during the fittings. The blue dresses looked alike at a glance but Aunt Grace made them so each flattered my cousins' very different figures. Kate almost looked pretty. My mom was a real angel about getting me married with a bit of Derby style. She never again mentioned anything about me becoming a nurse. She never again spoke of school or scholarships or university.

A few days after I told her about the baby and the wedding, and Nan was ordering the satin, the light went out of her eyes and she sat at the kitchen table and smoked, hardly eating, hardly saying a word. Then Flossie ran into the kitchen, gave Mom a big hug and Mom started chattering about what a lovely house I was going to have and wasn't Flossie going to be so smart with the books.

I felt her disappointment. My throat hurt with holding it all in. But that's what I did. It was no use crying a river or going over the what-ifs. We both knew that. We carried on, held our heads up high, like the strong Derby women we were supposed to be.

Rebecca was still hard to track down and I was so busy with the wedding that I had to let her be. I had no idea if she was going or staying. There was no more talk of a double wedding. I avoided being alone with Aunt Grace.

A week before the wedding I made one last attempt to find out what Rebecca was up to. I got more than I bargained for.

I went Down Below in the late morning and Rebecca was still in bed. She shouted down the stairs for me to wait in the parlor and to try a piece of music she had picked out for my wedding.

Before I sat down to play I took a long look at the painting of the stream flowing into the harbor. For the first time I looked real close in among the trees, and I could see a name. As clear as a lighthouse beacon, once you knew it was there. Henry Ellis, it said. A man with the same name as the one on Rebecca's birth certificate had his name signed to a painting right there in my aunt's home. He paints, Rebecca draws; how dumb could I have been not to make the connection earlier.

I stumbled over to the pictures set out on the tables. Normally I would never have touched them but this time my hand just shot out and picked up the one of Aunt Grace in her Red Cross uniform standing between two men, one in a suit and the other in a captain's uniform. Two of her patients, she always said. But there, scrawled across the back, in big bold handwriting, were the words, "To Grace, with all our love, Henry and Franklin." There was Henry again, a picture of him no less, in the parlor. A tall man and if I looked real hard I could make out a head of shining black hair and a perfect heart-shaped face. The Franklin was no other than Mr. Franklin Harris. You could just tell, if you knew what you were looking for. And the photo of Grace holding Rebecca as a baby—printed across the back was the name of a studio in Boston. My aunt was some bold.

I didn't wait for Rebecca to come down. I just left. And that very day Georgie and Flossie picked up the mail and I got a letter I'd been waiting for. I had got to convincing myself that Mr. Harris did know my aunt back in Boston and I got enough nerve to write him a letter. Yes, I did. I was real careful about copying out his address from the little card he had given me and I asked Charlie Mullen to mail it for me in the city. I said that I was sorry that the art school wasn't working out for Rebecca this summer and I left it hanging, suggesting that maybe it could happen next summer.

I got the most surprising letter back.

Dear Miss Garreaux,

It was very kind of you to write to suggest that perhaps your cousin Rebecca might be able to come to Boston next summer. That thought alone will get me through the long cold winter.

I've been Henry Ellis's friend since we were schoolboys. I was the best man at their wedding. Whatever your aunt should tell you, please remember that Henry has never forgotten his wife and daughter.

It took me a while to find Grace Ellis. Henry had written letters to her in Cook's Cove, even using her maiden name, but he didn't hear from her so we assumed she hadn't returned there. After checking every major city in Canada, I got a bee in my bonnet and decided this summer to come to see for myself.

There she was, as lovely as ever, raising on her own a beautiful daughter whose talent may well match her father's.

That's when I decided to try to lure Rebecca to Boston so she could see the kind of life she could have with the patronage of a loving father.

You are a very kind young woman to suggest that it may still be possible. I knew you had a warm heart the moment I met you.

Sincerely,

Franklin Harris

Later that night I went to my mother and I laid out everything I knew. I couldn't hold it in any longer and I hadn't promised Aunt Grace anything.

"You do see, don't you, Mom, that Rebecca has choices she doesn't know about?" I said. She didn't answer me right away.

I tried again. "This Mr. Harris took it for granted that we knew that Aunt Grace was married in Boston. He doesn't know about Uncle Wilf. By marrying her cousin and not changing her name, she had Mr. Harris believing she was all alone in the world."

She had left out the part of the story about marrying Henry Ellis. A missing piece fell into place. My aunt was a bigamist. This mess wasn't about keeping Rebecca in the Cove so Uncle Wilf could have a daughter to be proud of. It was about keeping him from ever finding out that Rebecca wasn't his daughter and that Grace wasn't his wife. It was about holding the shell of my aunt's life together.

As the dark grew deeper I made the case to my mom that next summer was our chance to get Rebecca out of the Cove and away from this life. Somehow, I said, we had to keep her away from Robert Gordon and get her to finish high school so she would be ready for whatever came her way.

My mom listened for the longest time and then she shushed me with a deep sigh. "Don't go on, my dear. We owe Grace too much to turn on her now." And that's when my mom told me about the time my aunt risked her life to save the both of us, my mom and me. She told me about it real slow.

My dad was in one of his bad moods. He'd drunk a whole bottle of moonshine and was getting rowdy. I was barely four years old. She couldn't remember what got him started but before she knew what was happening he was dragging her across the kitchen floor by her hair and I was in the corner, scared, staring at them. She tried to laugh to make it all seem like playtime between Mommy and Daddy. He wanted a mug of tea and he wanted it that instant. He was screaming at her and she got confused. She went to the storeroom to get some kerosene to help start the stove. Instead of kerosene she took the bottle of white gas. She splashed it into the stove and threw in a match. The stove went puff and the fire instantly licked onto the ceiling, the walls and the floor. When she turned around to shout for Roe to help her, he was gone.

There she was, in the middle of the kitchen with fire circling her and I was in the far corner, a wall of fire separating us. She tried to reach me but couldn't. There was no way through. Just when she thought she would walk through the flames and at least cover my body with hers, Grace came to the kitchen door. She'd seen Roe go along the road looking very agitated but he wouldn't say what was wrong.

Grace figured out in an instant what had to be done. She pushed the kitchen table into the middle of the room, through the fire, and ordered my mom to jump on top. No, my mom said, not without her baby. "You jump on right now and then we'll get Melinda. No one is leaving here without Melinda, do you hear me? Jump." My mom got on the table and listened hard as Grace told her she was going to push her and the table through the flames, that she was to grab me and then Grace would pull us both back.

My mom panicked. She couldn't concentrate. She could only see my big eyes looking at her through the fire. Grace yanked her off the table, pushed her away from the heat and then turned the table on its side and used it as shield to walk through the fire to pick me up. All three of us were out the door within seconds. All we salvaged from the kitchen was a bundle of family photos.

My mom was sobbing even as she remembered. "Don't you see, Melinda, I owe her one back, a big one. It took her almost a year to recover and she never told anyone. In all the fuss of saving the house, she just stole away to Down Below. She tended to the burns on her legs herself and wore heavy wool stockings all winter so no would know or ask questions. She never complained, not once. No one knows how Roe almost killed us both. I can't send her daughter away. I can't."

This was the last missing piece of the puzzle. That must have been the winter when I started spending so much time Down Below, and my aunt made me fudge every Sunday. My mom owed my Aunt Grace big time. A daughter for a daughter. It was a fair exchange.

I swallowed real hard and told my mom that I would do what had to be done to keep Rebecca here in the Cove.

❧

CHAPTER SIXTEEN

Six for gold

The last days leading up to my wedding were giddy. My Matt did the gyprock in the kitchen first and I was determined that one room would be pretty when we moved in. I painted every evening until I couldn't lift my arms one more time. The sunshine yellow was all the rage in the catalogue. I made blue gingham café curtains for the kitchen window, copied them from a picture in *Chatelaine* and I helped lay the blue and white linoleum. I waxed and polished the floor so you could eat off it and I put the set of dishes my mom gave us for a wedding present in the only cupboard we had.

I spent my days in the kitchen Upalong making up squares and cookies, mustards and relishes and streamers and roses to decorate the tables. I smiled at all the old biddies who repeated the old lore that a Saturday was just no day for a wedding while they took sneaky looks at my tummy.

On top of everything else there were three chores that begged to be finished up before the wedding.

The first was to go see Aunt Grace.

My wedding dress dragged a little in the back and Nan was up to her ears in pastry so she told me to take the dress down to Aunt Grace. After squeezing my way out of every chance to be alone with her for most of a month, on the Wednesday before the wedding I found her in her sewing room still working on the bridesmaid dresses; she with pins in her mouth, me with a tongue that must have been confused about why it was so still.

While she was on her knees doing the final check on the hem of my dress, I reached for my new black handbag and took out the envelope that had Rebecca's birth certificate in it. I handed it to her without a word. She didn't even look at it but slipped the envelope into her apron pocket and kept on pinning the hem. The strangest thing of all, she started to hum, and then sing, "Let Me Fish off Cape St. Mary's," an old Newfoundland ballad. I couldn't stop my voice from joining hers:

> When I reach that last big shoal
> Where the ground swells break asunder,
> Where the wild sands roll to the surges toll,
> Let me be a man and take it
> When my dory fails to make it.

I cried whenever I sang that verse. I used to think of my daddy, but standing there in my wedding dress I thought of my mother and her troubled life and dear dead Lottie and of me and Rebecca out there in that storm. It wasn't long before tears were streaming down my face and Aunt Grace was crying too. She crushed me in her arms.

"You're a good girl at heart, Melinda. You're very fortunate to be able to have the rest of your life with the man you love, always remember that," is what she said.

And I decided right there and then, while Aunt Grace was hugging me and letting me see into her heart, that I would talk to Rebecca the very next day.

I tracked her down in Robert's kitchen. She was just sitting on the daybed, popping bubbles, staring into space. For once in my life, my timing was right. After we'd talked a bit about the wedding cake she was decorating and the curtains I'd just put up at my house, she burst into tears.

Between the sobs she admitted that she only liked Robert when he wasn't home.

She hated the puzzled and hurt look she saw on her father's face. She couldn't stand not being able to talk to me and Kate the way she used to.

I wanted so badly to tell my cousin to leave, get out, go in the city with Kate and keep going, take a bus, get on the train, go to Boston, go to Toronto, don't even think about staying. Those words were in my brain but I barred them from my lips.

"You know, Rebecca, the big cities are not for you and me. You're just as rooted here as I am. We're two peas in a pod."

"But my life is too awful. Can you help me, Melinda? Come into Corner Brook with me in a couple of weeks and help me get the papers I need and find out about the train schedules. You'll be a married woman and people will believe you if you say my birth certificate was lost in a house fire. I could go away for a little while and learn more about drawing. I'd come back, you know, but I so want to go."

I asked the Lord for sweet mercy. I talked about how her dad needed her. I talked about how I needed her to be in the Cove so we could grow old together. I went on about how she could play the organ in church and be in charge of raffles. I said that by-and-by I would take over Aunt Grace's sick calls, but that she could do all the planning for the time and the garden party. I promised I would never tell a soul about when she was born and that her being a year older would be our secret forever. I told Rebecca her mom was real sorry about the mess she got us all in but that she was really only trying to protect the Derby name. I reminded her how she was the one who told Kate that life was miserable in the Cove for a fallen woman. And that Aunt Grace had a long way to fall. (And I made a promise to myself: Rebecca would never know that Uncle Wilf wasn't her father.)

It was a lot to say and I talked at her into the late morning saying the same things over and over, just differently, even convincing myself at times. I begged her not to destroy the family. I twisted that one so easily I felt myself blush with the shame of it.

And that shame pushed me to make one concession. I figured she was probably right about dumping old Robert. It was sad to see her jump at that. She wanted a way out and I gave it to her.

I got her a cold cloth for her eyes, and convinced her to go home and straighten her room, wipe off the makeup, get her schoolbooks ready. For all her being smart she still needed me to tell her what to do.

We would have some peace.

I went back Upalong to finish up a batch of rolls I had set to rise and to do the third thing that had to be done. I found some old fancy writing paper and wrote that Mr. Harris again. This time I told him that things had got unsettled in the Cove since I last wrote and that Rebecca had given up her drawing and had gone off to the mainland in a snit to be a hairdresser. My writing was big and black but I was deliberately vague.

To remind myself that I was a good person, I took a peek into the dining room at all the wedding gifts laid out on the table—the mixing bowls, tea towels, lace doilies, cushions, pretty bone china teacups and a fancy tray from Aunt Grace. That's when I started to cheer up.

Despite the old biddies we got a golden day for the opening of the road and my afternoon wedding. It was one of those rare September days with filtered sunlight and gentle sea breezes. In our Cove, September was unpredictable. There were often cold winds and sleet in August so we would batten down and then feel foolish when the winds sometimes turned warm and the sun washed the land, giving off a pinkish-yellow light that could last well into the balmy evening.

As soon as I woke up I ran my eyes over the white satin dress hanging on my closet door. Everything was in place; the veil hanging on a nail nearby, the shoes beneath the dress. I wanted to lie there forever and let the happiness reach the tip of my toes. But I could hear Nan and Mom down in the kitchen and there was still a lot to do.

I covered my hairpins with a fancy scarf, put on my new green dress and a big floursack apron. The turkeys still had to be cut and the gravy made, the last rolls put in the oven and the cookies and cakes put out on plates.

We got everything done that could be done and then, hardly wasting a step, we flung off our aprons, took out the curls, put on our shoes and raced up to the school for the eleven o'clock ribbon-cutting ceremony. Aunt Grace was sitting on the wooden riser decorated with Union Jacks. She was right up there with the reverend, our member of the legislative assembly and the Canadian minister of transportation, who were here to remind us where the construction money had come from.

There was no doubt that Aunt Grace was still reigning as the Lady of Down Below. She was wearing a new cherry-red suit and a white felt pillbox hat. She had ordered them special from Eva's Ladies' Shop in the city. I used to think the pearls she brought out for big occasions like this were from Woolworth's but I took a good look at them this time and decided that fake just wouldn't give off that soft sheen. She looked very respectable, sitting up there with all the officials, wearing Harry's pearls. She turned and gave me a soft smile.

The bigwigs wanted us to sing "O Canada" but none of us knew the words. We sang the "Ode to Newfoundland." There was loud applause and the ribbon was cut. Cook's Cove was no longer an isolated outport community on Newfoundland's west coast. No, we were the Cove at the beginning of the road around the Bay of Islands.

❧

CHAPTER 17

Seven for a secret that can't be told

I walked down the aisle of St. James's Church at four to become Mrs. Matt Lewis. I was carrying the same bouquet my mother had on her wedding day—the red roses from the climber out back. It was their second blooming and they were small but heavy with a sweet earthy perfume. Rebecca did them up. She had a real talent for knowing exactly how the roses should bunch and fall and she was an artist with the masses of bows and trailing white ribbons. My cousins carried smaller bouquets with blue ribbons and even little Flossie carried a basketful of buds.

We posed for lots of photos and it was my plan to pick out the nicest one for Aunt Grace's table. Rebecca went back to her drawing for the occasion and gave me a beautiful picture of me in my wedding dress that she'd done while she and Kate helped me get dressed. I couldn't believe that my eyes were shining like she did them but she said they were and Kate backed her up. I later framed it and hung it in our living room above the TV set.

The reception was a sit-down supper in the hall at the back of the school where all the weddings were held. I joked with my mom that I'd come back to school in September after all. She didn't even smile.

There was turkey and ham, potato salads, cole slaws, carrot salads and fancy dishes of homemade pickles, mustards and relishes. Rebecca had used almond paste to make dozens of tiny red rose buds for the bride cake and the roses were tied with real satin ribbons streaming down over the three layers. I couldn't eat, except for some squares and a tiny cut of pie.

Soon the tables were pushed back to make room for beer and dancing. I did a whirl around the floor with my husband and another with Uncle Wilf but the turning made me sick and I truly did not want to embarrass myself at my own wedding so I shooed my Matt off to join the fellas and I sat among the married women.

Mom had faded into the crowd but I picked her out because I knew all her hiding places. My eyes found her leaning into the doorway frame of the school kitchen almost lost in shadows. She was wearing the same navy dress she wore to everything special. The posy of roses and ribbons that Rebecca had done up for her was tucked into her collar but her sleeves were rolled up to the elbow. She had put herself in charge of cleaning the dishes.

She was thirty-four years old and so tired out that strangers took her for Grace's older sister. She was as thin as a sapling fir and if she didn't have a cigarette between her fingers she wouldn't know how to keep her hands still. The only time I saw her crack a smile was when she watched the twins walk up the aisle in front of me. Nan had made Flossie an adorable white dress from my scraps and trimmed it with lace. Flossie loved flouncing around in the layers of net, nylon and satin. She was going to be a beauty and a heartbreaker.

Nan turned an old blazer for Georgie and bought him gray flannels. My mom was so focused on those twins I had to nudge her elbow as I went by.

Aunt Grace had changed out of her red suit for the wedding. She looked lovely in a yellow dress. She was making the cousins from away feel welcome and telling everyone to come and eat some more. Earlier in the evening she had got up in front of everyone and did a little talk on how delighted the Derbys were to welcome my Matt into the clan. I don't think it crossed her mind that I was now a Lewis and had been a Garreaux.

Juanita Barnes and Charlie Mullen were cuddling in the corner. They announced the week before that they would be getting married the Wednesday after Christmas. That was the signal that she wasn't knocked up, four months to plan a perfect trip down the aisle. She had quit school and was working at the fish plant to pay for her wedding.

Mabel Smith's little boy Jimmy was running wild, jazzing when he sat down and scooting in and out among the dancers when Mabel wasn't looking. Mabel told him she was leaving him with his grandparents for a little while and he went on a tear right away. Since Mabel got to know Rebecca she toned down her colors and even lost a bit of weight. One of the young engineers who came to the Cove with the road bigwigs stayed on for the wedding and he couldn't keep his eyes off her. Maybe something good would come of the road sooner than we thought possible. She deserved a break.

Lottie's husband, Jamie, was drunk. His brothers and sisters had gone back to being a wild lot. Seeing them running all over the place reminded me that in the short time that Lottie was with them, she'd managed to teach them a few manners, now forgotten, and something about cleanliness, also gone by the by.

Kate and Chas were at opposite ends of the room. There was no chance that my Aunt Mary would get it into her head that Kate was in love with a fella from the Cove.

Chas was playing his accordion and Kate was with Uncle Wilf talking her head off about working harder to get her maths mark up. She did look nice though. Her cheeks were flushed a healthy pink, the blue dress matched her eyes and the tucks were in all the right places.

Just this afternoon she had done a good deed. While she was giving the parlor one last dusting, she "accidentally" knocked the Bible off the sideboard and out dropped the photo of the family with Edward on Nan's lap. It was black around the edges and my mom was almost burned off but Nan did a jig when Kate picked it up and handed it to her. It turned out that Kate had sneaked the photo out of the secret box the same time I took the birth certificate. I wondered if she would ever get up the nerve to tell Aunt Grace that the photo that Nan trimmed and was handing around to anyone who would look, was the one that used to be in her hideaway.

Robert Gordon was standing off to the side, absolutely never taking his eyes off Rebecca. She might have broken up with him on Thursday night but he hadn't broken up with her.

My cousin did me proud. It was her birthday but she was cheerfully helping Nan keep the food table full and disappearing into the kitchen occasionally to bring out a stack of freshly washed plates or a tray of glasses. The eyebrows were still arched but they were a little thicker—more natural. Her lipstick and nail polish had gone from bright red to a pearly pink. In between her kitchen duties she was making sure her dad had enough to eat and a full glass of beer at his elbow. Uncle Wilf beamed every time she went by in her long blue dress. He had his little girl back.

The music turned to a waltz. My Matt came from across the room to claim me for the dance. I reached down to touch my new gold band. I was sixteen years old and Mrs. Matt Lewis and we were having a baby in the spring.

I hoped for a girl, a girl who wouldn't make me a grandmother when I was thirty. Please, dear God. A girl who would use the new road to the outside world. And, I could only hope, be better for it when she came back to us.

I took my husband's arm. Oh, how we danced.

MARY C. SHEPPARD has been a journalist for twenty-five years and has worked at *Maclean's*, CBC Radio and WTN. She now teaches broadcast journalism at Ryerson Polytechnic University. From a family of nine children, Mary has one brother and seven sisters. She grew up in Corner Brook, Newfoundland, and spent most of her summers in an outport community very much like Cook's Cove.